# THE BLOOMING ROSE

## A Biography

**A tribute to** ROSE SIBUSISIWE MATUTU
1.3.1953 to 3.12.2007

## BY

## BRYAN MATUTU

Order this book online at www.trafford.com
or email orders@trafford.com

Most Trafford titles are also available at major online book retailers.

Note for Librarians: A cataloguing record for this book is available from Library
and Archives Canada at www.collectionscanada.ca/amicus/index-e.html

Printed in Victoria, BC, Canada.

ISBN: 978-1-4251-9075-0 (soft)
ISBN: 978-1-4251-9077-4 (e-book)

*Our mission is to efficiently provide the world's finest, most comprehensive
book publishing service, enabling every author to experience success.
To find out how to publish your book, your way, and have it available
worldwide, visit us online at www.trafford.com*

*Trafford rev.10/19/2009*

**North America & international**
toll-free: 1 888 232 4444 (USA & Canada)
phone: 250 383 6864 ♦ fax: 812 355 4082

# Preface

"Fear God and keep His commandments; for that is man's all." These profound words were said by the wisest man who ever lived, King Solomon, as recorded in the Book of Ecclesiastes, Chapter 12;13. After my dear wife, Rose *Sibusisiwe* MATUTU, departed from this wretched earth for her heavenly glory, I searched for an answer as to why God would visit me in such a severe manner. The comfort I got from the saints at Avondale Church of Christ, Harare, and the church in Zimbabwe as a whole, as well as my extended family, was a revelation that directed me back to the holy book in general and to the quoted passage in particular. The testimonies I heard during the five day funeral wake left me in no doubt that Rose had lived for her God and that God had a clear purpose in her life and in uprooting her "prematurely". Not that I needed any reminder, as I had witnessed it first hand. She "had fought a good fight and had finished her race" and would have by now received her crown of righteousness (2 Timothy 4:7, 8). I am convinced that she would have accomplished more had she lived beyond the 54 years that she did. Not that we are saved by our works, but indeed by grace, (Ephesians 2:8, 9). My only regret is that I did not appreciate her as much as I should have during the thirty years of our life together.

As I reflected on these testimonies, I committed myself to writing the story of my beloved Rose, **the Rose of roses, the rose that has always been in full bloom and that will remain so until Amen**; hence the title of this book. Whilst the garden rose is seasonal and, once cut, fades away, my own Rose remains eternal. Please note well that by referring to her as an angel in this book, I am not implying that she was a real heavenly angel but that she was an exceptionally good person who had a significant and positive influence on everyone she interacted with. Naturally, she had her shortcomings like every human being. Nonetheless, at times I am tempted to believe that she was a real angel from above for she was unique in several aspects.

It would be amiss for me to write her story without showing how she related with me during the 30 years we lived together; for that is the very basis of her story. Even as I write this book, I am still numb with grief. I pray to God that this be part of the healing process for me. I regret to advise that most of you, particularly those who have known me after I became a practicing Christian, will be surprised to read about the dark side of me. I do not regret letting you into my past for I am certain that the God of all grace has already forgiven me. However, because Rose loved me so much, she persevered and eventually won me over for Christ. My earlier association with the wrong company had a telling effect on our marriage as my values had been misplaced. As for her, she had one solution; she lived for her God first and her family second. Everything else followed. As I said at her burial, the Bible tells us that some people have entertained angels without recognizing them. Well, God gave me the honour and privilege to live with one for 30 years yet my eyes were completely shut, only to realize it after her departure. Much as it pained me to lose her, I do not take Rose as dead, she has simply departed for another world… another realm. By God's grace we shall meet again. In this book, I have therefore referred to her departure rather than her death as death has some sound of finality to it, yet she lives.

My first reason for writing this book is to confess before God and to the world that I am a sinner and I know that in his wisdom, he has already forgiven me for my transgressions. This is not a self condemnation but an acknowledgement that I found favour before God who gave me such an angel for a wife in spite of my sinful ways. I also pray to God that he fills the gap left by Rose, in his own way and in his good time, lest I fall apart. I avail myself to God so that he can work through me towards the attainment of his mission here on earth, in whatever capacity he may choose for me.

The second reason is to give readers an insight into Rose's life so that others, particularly those who had the privilege of knowing her, including my children, may learn from her and be encouraged on their sojourn on this wretched earth. Simply put, this is a tribute to a unique yet simple personality. It is by no means an attempt at a professional guide for anyone but if it happens that someone benefits form this book, let all glory be given to God.

Thirdly but by no means least, I write this book as a means of celebrating her unique life here on earth and her migration to the land of eternity where she is now in the arms of her Lord and Saviour.

To my children, *Tatenda* Bryan and his wife *Munyaradzi*, *Tafadzwa* Thelma, Kevin *Tawanda* and Lynda *Tariro*, this is the story of your mum and I pray to God that it will guide you positively for the rest of your lives, even well after I am gone. I am confident that although she left us 'prematurely', she had fully played her role as my soul mate and adequate helper as well as bringing you up as defined by the good Lord. God had a good reason to take her away at the time He did and who are we to question Him? This is why you were such a strong source of comfort for me during the hurting period. I just don't know how I would have coped without your company. I hope you will learn from your mum and that you will take after her and have Jesus Christ as your light, ALWAYS.

I have included a glossary of Zimbabwean vernacular words, including names, at the end of the book.

I pray that all those who read this book will be blessed.

All Bible quotations have been taken from The New King James version. The Bible passage references given at the end of some chapters are meant to buttress the general theme of the respective chapter while those given within the body of a given chapter are meant to support a specific point. Some of the verses are grouped in line with a common theme.

# Acknowledgements

My appreciation goes to all those who comforted me during my grieving period. I would also like to acknowledge, most gratefully, contributions made by the following bodies and individuals towards the writing of this book. I trust that those who may have also contributed but are not mentioned hereunder will not feel offended as this was purely an error of omission.

Mrs. Barbara Nkala and Mr. Edmund Chipamaunga for their patience and invaluable guidance and for proof reading my manuscript.

Mrs. Judith Chiume and Mrs. Molly Mtisi (both born Ngole)

The elders and ladies of Avondale Church of Christ

The Premier Services Medical Aid Society

Mr. Fani Wesley Sibanda (Sebatha)

My brothers in Christ, Eubert Mashaire and Never Sibanda

All those who consoled me by their presence and by their testimonies during the grieving period. I also received a number of books on how to handle grief which I found most invaluable.

# Dedication

This book is dedicated to my children;
Tatenda Bryan,
Tafadzwa Thelma,
Kevin Tawanda and
Lynda Tariro
As well as my grandson, Ethan Tatenda

# Contents

## SECTION THREE

## REFLECTIONS

# SECTION ONE

## IN THE FLESH

# 1

## The Angelic Cradle

Two young men, Ntuta Tom Ngole Mokoena and Wesley Sebatha left their homes in what is now Lesotho in the mid 1800s and headed for what is Botswana today. They settled in the Ramakwebana area before crossing into Plumtree, Zimbabwe, where they settled for some years. The two gentlemen were later to become the pioneers of Bulawayo where they eventually settled by the turn of the century. Having settled among the Ndebeles, the two adopted the Ndebele versions of their names in order to fit into that community and became known as Ngwenya and Sibanda respectively

By 1904, Missionaries of the Associated Churches of Christ from Australia/New Zealand had started what was then known as Intini Mission which was located somewhere between Hillside and Matsheumhlope suburbs of Bulawayo. The two gentlemen joined the mission in 1905 as newly converted Christians and were later trained as teachers and preachers of the word of Christ. They were so well grilled in the Queen's language to the extent that they later became reference points regarding the language after moving to Zvishavane. To this day, their descendants have been known for their eloquence in the English language with a number of them having been prominent teachers. These were sons Daniel Ngole and Henry Ngole as well as some of their grandchildren who later taught at Dadaya and Nhowe Missions in the 1950s and 1960s. From the Sibanda line come Fani Wesley Sibanda and Timothy Sibanda, among others, all of whom have also been known for their eloquence in English language. In 1907, Wesley Sibanda was dispatched to start Lundi Primary School while Tom Ngole was to later start Rusvinge Primary School, both in the Zvishavane area. In 1945, the two men and their families relocated to Mbilashaba Primary School which is located 12 kilometres from Zvishavane along the Gweru road.

Ngole and his wife, *Gogo MaNdlovu*, eventually had five girls and five boys. It was their second born daughter, Nellie, who was to become the grandmother of the subject of this book through her own daughter, Emmie *Ncube (uMaNcube)*. Readers may be wondering why I am giving Rose's maternal genealogy and not that of her father. This is the only traceable line available to me as Rose never knew her father although she knew his name to be Stanley Tazvishaya of the *Mhofu/Mpofu totem*. She neither had the opportunity to know his people nor where he came from.

Rose *Sibusisiwe* was born at Pikiri Village, Chief Masunda, in the district of Zvishavane in the southern part of Zimbabwe on 1 March 1953. Born to a single mother, she spent her childhood under the tutelage and disciplinary hand of *Gogo* MaNdlovu, her maternal great grand-mother. Of *Gogo* MaNdlovu's great-grand children, Rose became the closest and was like her own child. Although Tatenda was not Gogo's first great great-grand child, his arrival was a special occasion for her. MaNcube had two of her mother's brothers, Daniel and Henry who, with their wives, also played significant roles in the bringing up of Rose. MaNcube had been born in Gwatemba, Matabeleland South, but was also brought up by *Gogo* MaNdlovu where Rose would later be born and raised. Rose therefore assumed the Ngwenya/Ngole name from birth.

**It was *Gogo* MaNdlovu who played a major role in instilling discipline and the values that would guide Rose later in her adult life.** *Gogo's* mentorship would have a life long effect on Rose as reflected throughout this book. In later years Rose would talk fondly of the good moments she had shared with *Gogo* back then. She would mention how on many nights she failed to sleep as *Gogo* often woke up at night to heat up her kettle of tea for another cup. It was then that Rose learnt that old people have very little sleep. There were also occasions when *Gogo* would be furious with the girls after finding out that they had cooked and eaten fish, which was forbidden in their home because of their *Ngwenya totem* (see totem under Glossary on why fish was forbidden). Despite *Gogo's* unwavering care and love, not living with her own parents had a telling effect on Rose as she developed a habit of dropping her head to the side in self pity, a habit which earned her the nickname *Sitshekwana*. Many of her contemporaries believed this to be her real name.

Her mother was then very active in the liberation struggle nationalist politics together with her aunt, Lizzie *Ngole,* later married to Mr. Chirwa of Malawi. Both were detained by the government of Ian Douglas Smith, the Prime Minister of what was then Rhodesia, on a number of times. Relations between mother and daughter were often characterized by prolonged separations and irregular reunions until Rose's return from Malawi in the early 1970s (see chapter 2). Later in life the two appeared to have struggled to bond, as their values were somewhat at variance, until about four years prior to Rose's departure when Rose went out of her way to reach out to *Amai* (MaNcube) and started to buy groceries for her and to pay her monthly rentals. Earlier, *Amai* had declined our offer for her to occupy our backyard cottage. In retrospect, it is now clear that the rapprochement was in preparation for Rose's departure.

Rose and I started formal school together in 1959 at Mbilashaba Primary School, less than a kilometre from her home. She was a slim and reserved girl then and was just one of the many Ngwenya/Ngole girls at the school among whom were Molly, Judith, Caroline, Sheila and others. I was equally thin and came from a poorer background where education was hardly valued. The Ngoles were an influential family in the area in terms of wealth and education. Their connections with the local church also gave them special status as the community generally looked up to them for guidance in several aspects of life.

That early in life, neither of us ever dreamt that our lives would meet in future, let alone that we were destined for each other. However, as we progressed in primary school I began to notice her but not for her character or beauty. We were competitors of a kind in class. She was very good in English language and not quite so good in Mathematics while it was the exact opposite for me. The year end success ratings were largely influenced by results in either of these two subjects and we always competed for positions within the top five best students in class. However, after nearly failing my English language examination at Junior Certificate level, both my spoken and written language took a significant turn for the better at Ordinary Level, thanks to my then English teacher, author and later Zimbabwean ambassador to the United States of America and Kenya, His Excellency Edmund O. Chipamaunga. One characteristic which I noticed in Rose then was her humility and shyness which many of the uninitiated always mistook for *kupusa*. In this respect we were very much alike as many of my school mates used to laugh at me as well, thinking I was stupid. I would tease them back by saying that I did not mind being stupid if that meant that I was always ahead of them in class. Naturally, this would draw some long faces, especially from the older boys. Except for our different exposures in adult life, neither of us changed much.

The values of the African extended family system, though with some drawbacks, are fully demonstrated in the early part of Rose's life. To think that Rose was brought up by her mother's grandmother and turned out to be such a fine product speaks volumes for the Ndebele/Shona culture. On her part, she did not let adversity discourage her. To the contrary, it became the bedrock of her character for she was hardened in the right direction.

Reference passages; Proverbs 3:1, Jeremiah 1:5, Isaiah 49:1-2, Exodus 33:12 and Luke 1:15

# 2

## Education and Dating

After Standard Three, now Grade 5, (we did two sub standard years before starting standard one then) her mother, who then stayed in Salisbury (now Harare) moved Rose to Dadaya Mission for the rest of her primary school and I didn't see her for the following seven years. I even forgot all about her. Unfortunately for me, (even though she didn't mean much to me then), when I moved to Dadaya for my Form One in 1968, the bird had flown away. She had moved to Malawi where she stayed with Mr. and Mrs. Banda before eventually moving in with her mother's aunt, Mrs. Lizzie Chirwa who had then migrated to Malawi. In order for her to start school in Malawi, Rose had to change her identity to that of a Malawian and became firstly, Rose Banda and later Rose Chirwa, as many of her early adult friends back in Zimbabwe would know her later. She did her two years of secondary school and trained as a Medical Assistant (later to be known as State Certified Nurse) at Likuni Mission Hospital outside Lilongwe in Malawi. It was in between the two years of secondary education and the nurse training in 1970 that she came back home and I believe it was no accident that we met, for that day was to chart the course for the rest of our lives. We met at a Sunday church service at Mbilashaba School and during the service I kept glancing at her, amazed at how she had transformed during the preceding seven years. She also kept stealing a glance at me now and then although I did not know why. 'Would she remember me,' I wondered. I was then in Form Three at Dadaya and had physically transformed in my own way although I had retained my lanky features. After service, I had to find ways of pulling her away from *Gogo* MaNdlovu, her mentor. I had to be aggressive and my first expression was; "Wow, you have been transformed; what happened to you?" She smiled and we exchanged greetings. By then, her beautiful smile was characterized by long incisor like front teeth and that smile was to become one of her peculiar features in adult life.

Of course, she had not forgotten me. Although she was still tall, she had started filling up and the thinness was noticeably reduced and the beauty which had been latent was now clearly evident. She was now more confident and had developed that infectious smile. We had a good chat and exchanged addresses. I persuaded her to let *Gogo* and the other ladies go so that I could walk her home but she would have none of that. "What would *Gogo* think of me," was her response.

Although I did not lose hope, I went home with mixed feelings having been encouraged by the warmth that had been evident between us. Something told me that she was meant for me but the distance between us was to become a source of discouragement. After all, we were still in our teen years and too young for a serious relationship.

Back at Dadaya, I wrote her a letter proposing love. My father who had earlier been a "lay" preacher in the church had named me Ananias, although I am not sure which of the several Biblical characters I was named after among the liar, the high priest and the disciple of Damascus who prayed for Saul of Tarsus to regain his sight. The naughty ones among my contemporaries used to sing a derogatory song about Ananias and Sapphira whenever they saw me. This contributed to my disliking this name, and I opted for my middle name, Bryan, and this is the name many friends and acquaintances have known me by since then.

Her reply was not long in coming but contained no good news. She stated bluntly but politely that she had someone else in her life but suggested that we remain friends. I was despondent and saw no point in further distant correspondence with someone who was not a prospect but something within me told me, yet again, that she was special and was going to be my wife although I had no idea how this would come about.

Meanwhile, prospects for my own education had looked bleak after my father had seriously taken to drinking, lost his job as a land surveyor's assistant and had all his cattle killed by the severe drought of 1968. My maternal uncle, *Tyanai Chingarande,* had just started work as a general hand with the national railways company and he gladly offered to sponsor my secondary education after noticing my good grades at Standard Six. I have ever remained grateful to him and his dear wife, Lois, for their generosity. In retrospect, I now look at God's providence with fond memories. I had always come among the top in Arithmetic (Mathematics) but due to a misunderstanding of the invigilator's instructions when writing my Standard One year end examinations in 1961, I only jotted down the answers without showing the workings. Needless to say, although the answers were correct, I failed the exam and had to repeat the class the following year. God's providence comes in that my uncle only started working in 1967, the final year of my revised primary schooling. Had I not failed Standard One, I would have completed primary school in 1966 when my uncle was unemployed and clearly would have ended my formal schooling then. No doubt I would not have become what I am today. In those years, it took a lot of insight and dedication for someone to succeed through informal education channels. Chances of proposing to Rose would have also probably been minimized. 'Thank you, gracious God, for my silly mistake way back in 1961.'

For six years Rose and I neither met nor corresponded and I completely forgot about her. It was in 1976 when I was a bank teller in Bulawayo, when one evening, after boarding my bus back home at the old Lobengula Bus Rank (corner of Sixth Avenue) that I couldn't believe my eyes. There, walking past my window was Rose. I quickly disembarked, the bus fare already paid was of no value now, and followed her to her ticket line. On seeing me she simply exclaimed "B!" and hugged me. This was to be the affectionate name she would call me by until God separated us in 2007, 31 years later. Otherwise, from that early in our relationship we have rarely, if ever, called each other by our first names, preferring to call each other simply "Love". What an exciting moment this was for both of us. The rest is history as the expression goes. However, on the occasions I recounted this story to others later in our lives, Rose would be a bit uncomfortable as she somehow felt that the story made her look a bit cheap, being the conservative person she always was. I always assured her that I was comfortable retelling our story as it defined who we were. The truth is that we fell madly in love the moment we saw each other on that blessed day and nothing could take that away from us. I just don't know who fell harder. In fact, I think it was the resumption of the then undeclared love that was nonetheless evident at Mbilashaba in 1970.

Rose was now working as a nurse at a local polyclinic in Mzilikazi Township. She occupied a room at a house near her work place to which she never invited me. My friends would laugh at me saying that she could have been staying with a man but I knew better. It was simply because she did not want us to be tempted to do the wrong things and I gladly went along with her wishes; not that I would have succeeded if I had insisted on visiting her, for she always knew what she wanted. I remember one afternoon when we visited a local park and I managed to kiss her on the lips and her whole body resonated with excitement, like I had never seen in a woman. She mentioned to me that this was because she had never kissed a man, let alone gone to bed with one. This had therefore been the closest that she had ever got to a man. I was impressed. She was now 23 years old while I was a year older.

Heartbreak would follow. I was now a reckless and adventurous young man who had already dated and slept with a number of girls. Although I had been baptized into the church in high school, I had fully departed from the faith that defines us as Christians. Whilst I knew she was special, I expected her to behave like the other girls I had dated. She would not take any of that and a sharp difference arose that eventually led to us parting ways. Her position was simply that I should wait for our wedding day if I really loved her. I remember one afternoon when she visited me at home and we had a good time together. When she realized I was a bit drunk and wanted to cross the line, she got furious and immediately left. What had started as a beautiful day ended with me trying to physically drag her back home. I only stopped when she started screaming and a number of people from the neighbourhood started watching, wondering what was going on. I was ashamed to escort her to the bus stop and thus we parted our ways for some months. Once again, my sixth sense told me she was special and was mine. It took a tragedy to reunite us. A few months later, a friend of mine, Sydney, who was lodging at my house died in a road traffic accident, the same means by which she was later to leave me, and she came for the burial. From there she agreed to accompany me home and we resumed our relationship. Thanks to her patience. This proved to me that even though she disapproved of my earlier behaviour, she loved me deeply, just as much as I did.

After marriage, Rose started improving herself academically. She started studying for her Ordinary Level qualification. As mentioned earlier, she was not strong in Mathematics but with my help she persevered and eventually passed. The perseverance once again proved to me that Rose was no ordinary person. She then enrolled for and completed the General Nursing qualification as an improvement on the State Certified course that she had. She went on to study for Advanced level and passed well, once again with my assistance, especially in subjects requiring mathematical calculations. By the time of her departure, Rose was in her final year of a degree in Psychology with the Zimbabwe Open University. Despite struggling with the mathematics modules, she persevered and was doing her research paper when she passed on. Only determination and perseverance could have taken her thus far. This was another dominant trait throughout her life as she always thrived against any odds that would appear in her way.

Rose deferred fully to her mentor and great grandmother, showing that she always thought of other people, how her actions would affect them and how they would view those actions. In short, she was consistently considerate in all her actions. Rose hated taking life for whatever reason even that of animals, probably with the exception of a snake, For instance, she always ran away when a chicken or goat was being slaughtered. She would rather eat vegetables than slaughter a chicken. Of course, she would eat the meat as long as she was not involved in the slaughter. This trait remained evident in adult life. Her interests became subordinated to those of others. Exceptions are, however, noted.

Reference passages; Exodus 20:12, Prov 22:6, Eph 6:2-3, Acts 9:36, 39 and Gal 6:9

# 3

# The Ngole Family Perspective

This chapter was contributed by Mrs. Judith Chiume, born Ngole, on behalf of the Ngole Ngwenya family to whom I am truly indebted. Mrs. Chiume was daughter of the late Mrs. Lizzie Ngole Chirwa who at one time stayed with Rose in Malawi.

*Indeed Rose was a candle in the wind, not only to the Ngole family but also to all those who knew her. To the Ngole Ngwenya family where Rose was born and brought up, her departure has been a terrible blow that those of us remaining will find hard to come to terms with. We all know that it is a journey none of us can avoid but the wound her departure has left in us all, only the mighty physician, Lord Jesus, will heal.*

*As we were growing up with Rose, she showed very unique and remarkable qualities that left an indelible mark in us all. Now that she is gone, I can see that these were meant for us to learn from. Rose was an outstanding and influential character to her peers and adults alike. Even the hard hearted among us found it difficult to be unkind to Rose. The best one could do was to reciprocate her own love and kindness which she always exuded. She related well with* all the relatives in the Ngwenya clan without exception throughout her life.

Rose was a very quiet but dependable... well disciplined, kind, loving, very industrious and a God loving person. Most of our peers in the family were fond of bad conduct and were often unruly and had self inflicted teenage problems to which Rose was the only exception. Small wonder God blessed her with an outstanding married life and precious children.

Her mentor as she was growing up was ugogo, Mrs Ngole Ngwenya (uMaNdlovu) from whom I have no doubt Rose drew her meek personality, notwithstanding that she was of the fourth generation from ugogo. Rose's financial and material needs were well catered for by her mother, and my cousin, Emmie, as she was growing up. Uncle Daniel Ngole was her pillar of strength as he filled the fatherly role she would have otherwise missed as she never knew her father. Uncle Daniel loved all of us without any discrimination of any kind but was particularly very close to Rose, although we initially did not understand why. Matters became clearer as we grew up and started to appreciate things differently.

Rose went to school at Mbilashaba and Dadaya primary schools before moving to Malawi for her junior secondary school and nursing at Likuni Mission. There she was loved by all people she came into contact with and cared for patients in a particularly remarkable and impressive manner. The hospital matron at that time, a Roman Catholic nun, confided to my late mother that Rose had a unique gift that she had never seen in any one else in all her nursing career. Rose displayed characteristics of a great counsellor and was an amazing comforter with a touch of immense healing to the wounded spirit of both patients and staff alike. This matron, whose name I regrettably cannot recall now, appeared to have taken over from ugogo, uMaNdlovu, as Rose's mentor. Rose always had fond memories Of the values she had always (The author can confirm that the chastity vows and other values that guided Rose's life were, to a great extent, learnt from this matron. Rose used to speak fondly of this matron, whose name I also cannot remember.)

*Although I was slightly older than Rose and was in a position of authority as her aunt, I found it difficult to lord it over her. Instead I often found myself deferring to her for counsel and guidance. In her adult life there seemed to have been a thorn in her life that I do not want to talk about as I do not understand at times what fate brings in a person's life. God gave Rose the courage to deal with the thorn throughout her life. Rose was a cheerful and wonderful giver. In most cases, her gifts were not huge but precious little things that came from deep within her heart and that would be difficult to forget. To cap it, she was always cheerful, even when something was bothering her.*

*In our adult life, distance became a huge setback as I stayed in Malawi and later in South Africa while she remained in Zimbabwe. The welcome I always received when I visited her home confirmed to me that she had not changed from being the warm embracer of all those who needed her precious heart of unconditional love. Truly, Rose was a remarkable and rare personality who has left a gap which many of us will never dream of filling. We simply do not know how she did it.*

*May the good Lord give comfort and rest for her beautiful soul. I would like to remind Bryan and the children of what God said to Joshua (Joshua 1: 5) after the departure of Moses and that they may also be comforted by these words. "No man shall be able to stand before you all the days of your life; as I was with Moses (Rose) so I shall be with you. I will not leave you nor forsake you."*

# 4

# Marriage

When *Amai* named her Sibusisiwe, she was acknowledging the blessing that came with a new born baby girl. Little did she know that this was a prophecy intended more for me as her future husband; for indeed, most, if not all, of the blessings were reserved for me.

At the age of twenty four, Rose was still a virgin and had vowed only to concede after our wedding. However, after some months of dating following our reunion, she succumbed and became pregnant with our first child, *Tatenda* Bryan. We had to quickly formalize the situation by identifying a *munyai/idombo* to approach her guardian, *Sekuru* Henry Ngole. I was soon accepted as a *mukwasha/umkhwenyana*. I was now part of the Ngwenya family as much as she was part of the Matutu family. Tatenda was born on 30 June 1978 and there was great happiness in the Matutu extended family. I was a first born son to a first born father and a first born mother. Tatenda was therefore a first born son to first born parents and first born grandparents and was the very first of a new Matutu ( *Ndlela)* generation who was destined to carry the family name: 'the crown prince' as it were. Tatenda was to later get married to Munyaradzi, another first born. Although there may be no specific relevance, it is interesting to note that the lineage of first borns has been maintained with the birth of Ethan to Tatenda and Munyaradzi on 20 January 2009.

The birth of Tatenda gave Rose a special position in the family and all eyes were focusing on her as she became known simply as *Mai Tatenda* or *MaMpofu*. She did not disappoint us as she endeared herself with everyone due to her personality. In later years, she was to fulfil that role commendably well. On 20 March 1981, we formally got married at the Harare Magistrate Court followed by a wedding ceremony. By this marriage she had assumed a new and permanent name unlike the Ngwenya, Banda, Chirwa and Mpofu names she had carried in the past. This must have been a load she was keen to shed, once and for all. She had adopted the Mpofu name on our wedding invitation cards in search of her true identity. She was to carry the Matutu name with pride and distinction in years to come. We were later blessed with three other children, *Tafadzwa* Thelma in 1982, Kevin *Tawanda* in 1984 and Lynda *Tariro* in 1986.

It has been observed that in many cultures across the world, there is always an undeclared war between a mother-in-law and her daughter-in-law. Zimbabwe is not an exception in this aspect. Although this feud surfaced on some occasions between Rose and my mother, it was not much as the two quickly established some rapport. However , I remember one incident when mother visited us after we had refurnished our little house in Luveve Township in Bulawayo. After inspecting the quality of the furniture (in our absence) she was heard to complain that Rose was influencing me to buy a timber framed bed rather than a metal one; the supposition being that metal was more durable than wood. Rose took exception to that and for some time relations were a bit strained although Rose would try to hide it. Mother also took time to let go of me as somehow Rose was like an intruder into our relationship. Thanks to the effort of both parties, the feud never grew to levels that have been noted in many families. In fact, their relations were extremely good and mother would later express how she was extremely impressed by Rose and to have a *muroora* like her.

Unfortunately some disappointments were in store for Rose. Whilst I loved her most dearly, like I had never loved anyone before her, I still went out with other girls. My values were still skewed and I was very slow to mature. Nineteen eighty two was a devastating year for her. We were then staying in Gwanda, a town in south western Zimbabwe, when I fell for a young girl who later became pregnant with my child. Ironically, Rose used to give extraordinary care to this girl, as per her normal practice, whenever the latter visited the local hospital for her ante-natal routines. To say that Rose was disappointed when she discovered this relationship is an understatement. She simply went numb with disbelief. For a good three hours she cried uncontrollably and I did not know what to do. She then disappeared for about an hour during which time I had no idea of her whereabouts. I remained helpless in the house with little *Tafadzwa* who was a few months old then. When I later told her upon her return that I was worried that she would commit suicide she defiantly stated that she would never deliberately sin against God. She told me that she had just been wandering, confused. After her return, she cried for the whole night, literally. She couldn't accept, and rightly so, that after keeping herself pure for me, this was the reward she was getting. The perfect marriage she had envisaged and dreamt of had vanished before it ever started; a mirage never to be grasped. She also looked back at the special treatment she had been giving to this girl and agonized at the cruel irony of it all. Rose never accepted that the child from the extra marital relationship was mine as she was convinced that any woman who slept with a married man could not be faithful to that man and therefore anyone else could have been the father of that child.

In later years, she would be equally furious whenever the subject of the child somehow cropped up. The incident had left her heart broken and she never fully recovered from that state despite my concerted attempts to reason with her and the demonstrated change in my conduct. She remained suspicious of my movements. Up to the day of her departure, she could not accept that child as mine, let alone the concept that the child could come and stay with us one day. However, somehow I have a feeling she wanted to give the matter the benefit of the doubt but instead opted for a permanent denial which became her fall back position whenever the matter arose. She never accepted my argument that it was not the child's fault that she was born out of wedlock and that she was entitled to know her real father. She would rationalize by saying that she had been born in similar circumstances but had never sought her father and had no intention of meeting him as she knew she was an illegitimate child. At one time she used very strong words to describe the circumstances under which she was conceived. While I empathized with her, I had a feeling that she was not being quite honest otherwise she would not have used the Mpofu name at the time that she did. However, I never reminded her of this lest I would hurt her more when she was already the victim.

My defence was that having an extra marital affair did not mean I did not love her. She never accepted this line of rationalization. She strongly insisted that I did not love her otherwise I would not be unfaithful, for no person can love two people equally at the same time. When at one time I visited the girl's parents to pay "damages" (compensation paid to parents of a girl made pregnant by someone who has no intention of marriage), Rose became equally furious as she concluded that I had gone to formalize marriage arrangements despite my assurances to the contrary. She could not imagine herself in a polygamous marriage. Subsequently, a girl child was born to the other woman

who named her *Kwazinkosi(Kwazi)*, for only the Lord could solve
the mother and child's problems and knew what was in store for
them. In due course, the other woman got married and I am
truly grateful to her husband for bringing up my child. I am yet
to meet this man.

After a number of years and following heated debates, Rose
agreed that Kwazi could come and stay with us but reversed her
position at the point of implementation having given the matter
a second thought. At another time she agreed that we could
arrange for a blood test to verify if the child was mine but once
again she later changed position on the premise that there was no
need for us to incur unnecessarily heavy costs as such a test would
only confirm a probability rather than a certainty. Although her
argument was technically correct, I strongly felt that she was
afraid the test would confirm paternity. After yet another heated
debate Rose agreed that I could finance Kwazi's education and
upkeep, only for her to later deny that she ever consented. She
made no secret of her fears that Kwazi would be a claimant to
my estate, to which she had tirelessly contributed, in the event
that I died before her. The fear of Kwazi possibly sharing equally
with Rose's children and of her possibly sharing her portion with
her mother was a source of nightmares for Rose. The thought of
Kwazi and her mother seated among the mourners at my funeral
drove her into frenzy. I found her hard line approach to this issue
rather contradictory to her other traits that presented her as a
kind and loving person. Whilst she was entitled to be hard with
me, I had expected her motherly instinct to dictate a different
approach to the matter. My options were clear but each had severe
consequences. I was torn between forcing matters by bringing
Kwazi home on one hand and preserving my marriage on the
other. I chose the latter, tough as it was. With passage of time,
I learnt to accept her point of view and began to appreciate her
more although this left me in a quandary.

Years later, Rose would still assume that I had met the child's mother whenever I visited Bulawayo on business. To Rose, assumption was just as good as fact and no amount of argument or persuasion would make her see otherwise. Although I admitted having met Kwazi, Rose strongly believed that I still had a relationship with the mother despite my protestations to the contrary. She would even go for days without talking to me, although she was always magnanimous and would continue to cook and wash for me. This could have been the thorn in the flesh that she shared with her aunt, Mrs. Judith Chiume, as captured in Chapter 3.

Clearly, this matter had a telling effect on our marriage as it was clear that Rose always had a lingering feeling that always inhibited her happiness. There were moments when she would try to go out of her way to please me but somehow fell short and I could always tell something was weighing her down. In fact, she was never fully convinced of my fidelity. With time, matters improved significantly, probably because she realized that I really loved her although full potential was never attained. Suffice it to say that we never had the marriage bliss she had dreamt of in her childhood and which we both deserved. On my part, the hands of time could not be turned back so that I could start all over again.

Reference passages; 2 Tim 2:1, 1 Corinth 16:13 and Prov 12:4

# 5

## Divine Intervention

In 1982 we moved to Marondera, a town seventy five kilometres south east of Harare. The Gwanda episode had brought some reformation on my part although Rose remained suspicious of my movements. One evening I went to the local bar and she telephoned me on the hotel bar phone so that she could invite me back home for dinner. Unfortunately, when I got to the phone, it got disconnected and I never knew who had phoned me. On my return home, despite my assurances that I had been at the hotel and had missed her telephone call, she insisted I had been elsewhere with a woman. An argument ensued. In my selfish and chauvinist view, she was being rude to me and I slapped her once. She slapped me back and in turn I hit her with a fisted hand on the forehead. She passed out...I panicked and called an ambulance. She only came to at the local hospital. This is the hospital where she worked and had a number of friends. One can imagine the embarrassment and agony she went through while being attended to by her workmates and friends. On her return home the following day she went out of her way to be nice and apologized for having suspected infidelity on my part. I was humbled by her magnanimity because there had been an historic basis for her suspicions. This incident remained an albatross around our necks for the duration of our marriage.

We quickly made up and a significant improvement in our relationship ensued. Rose then started to attend the local Church of Christ and although she invited me a number of times, I was not yet ready for the change. However, a new chapter had been opened in our lives. Kevin Tawanda was conceived soon afterwards, in the excitement of the improved relations.

Nineteen eighty three saw us moving to the central city of Kwekwe after another transfer there by my employers. I would drop and pick her from church regularly. No major incidents arose there. This is where Kevin Tawanda was born, at a private clinic in Redcliff.

In 1985 we moved back to the east, this time to Rusape, a town 170km south east of Harare. My behaviour saw further improvements and by then I was taking less alcohol. However, Rose had by now become more assertive and could not be ignored. She had always appealed to me to stop drinking but the change was occasioned more by health considerations than by her appeals. My family has a history of hyper acidity associated with gastritis going back to my grandfather down to my children. It is in this light that I have discouraged my children from drinking and smoking as I know that it would physically destroy them. I have never smoked, mainly for the same reasons. It is ironic that I am allergic to smoke yet I grew up in a smoke filled hut. I cannot even eat bacon and other smoked foodstuffs. I stopped drinking altogether in 1986, the year Lynda was born, although occasionally I take a glass of wine or two.

I would drop Rose for church service every Sunday morning and pick her up later. This became the turning point of my life and ultimately for the whole family. The local Church of Christ minister, Brother T Madanhi, would reason with me on a number of times about the virtues of being a follower of Christ. He was a very fine gentleman who liked me as a son and who gave me a lot of advice and encouragement about life in general. Between him and Rose they convinced me to rededicate myself to Christ. I am happy that this eventually happened and I was able to recommit myself to Christ. Since then, I am proud to say that, while I remain a sinner, the Lord Jesus Christ has been gracious to me and has been my guide when faced with difficult situations. Many a times I have found myself miraculously saved from life threatening situations where I would clearly see the heavy presence of God's hand. On at least three occasions, while with my family in our family motor vehicle, we were miraculously saved from what could have been fatal accidents. In each case, it was the other driver's miscalculation and the difference between life and death was probably a fraction of a second. Although we always took these near misses as miracles, I never fully gave credit to God, ascribing our fortune to luck. Only in later years, when recounting these incidences to others, did I realise that God indeed loves me and my family and that his hand has always been with us.

Although Rose appeared like a paradox at times, and left me rather confused on many occasions, she was in fact very consistent. She entertained no nonsense when it came to morals and laziness and was an angel with regards to kindness and love. It was an interesting and unique balancing act. She would simply not tolerate nonsense while in the next instance she would display her unflinching devotion and love.

Despite her strong will power and in spite of my weaknesses, Rose continued to minister to me as her husband and at no time did she contemplate divorce as a solution. Although she had every reason to file for divorce she chose otherwise. Considering her strong views on my infidelity, and that of anyone for that matter, I have never been able to understand why she chose to stay. It could have been because she did not want her children to experience the semi orphan-hood that she had gone through or simply her desire to make the marriage work. I will never know.

In many families, a quarrel or misunderstanding of this nature is followed by a dysfunctional family with one or both parties either neglecting their duties or doing them grudgingly or worse still, going their separate ways. This tends to happen when we think that we, and not God, have the answers to our problems. Not so with my Rose. May her soul find eternal peace.

We were staying in Rusape when Lynda *Tariro* was born in 1986 at a private hospital in Mutare. I had been content with three children but she prevailed upon me to have a fourth one. What a lovely one she turned out to be. All, except *Tatenda* Bryan, were delivered through caesarean section, indicating the sacrifices she went through for the sake of these children. Lynda Tariro was to be the last born although Rose never opted for permanent methods of family planning in case of an unforeseen tragedy; always the cautious one

In 1988 we moved yet again, this time to the brighter lights of the capital city of Harare. We immediately placed our membership at Avondale Church of Christ where we have remained until Rose's departure. However, in 1993 we briefly located to Nairobi, Kenya, and worshipped at Nairobi West's Great Commission Church of Christ. Before we returned to Harare by end of 1994, I had been ordained as an elder. Back home, I was once again ordained an elder at Avondale on 30th of May 1999, two days after my forty seventh birthday. I remain in that office as of today. However, the matter of Kwazi was not brought to the attention of the church at the appropriate time because Rose did not want it to be discussed, mainly because she never accepted that the former was my child. I do admit that I could have taken a firmer position on the matter but being the 'softie' that I think I am, I went along with her wishes. At the time of writing, the matter had been discussed with the elders at Avondale. Kwazi has since visited us twice, has met with Lynda and has spoken with her other half siblings on the phone. All of them appear to have accepted her although with some reservations, initially. On her part, she was pleasantly surprised when the hostile reception she had anticipated from them did not materialize. "My apprehension had been misplaced," she later told me. To this day lines of communications are wide open between her and her half siblings and I trust that with time, they shall fully bond.

Reference passages; Gen 2:18, 20, Prov 31:10-27, Luke 6:33,

# 6

# The Daughter

As already mentioned, Rose was an only child. The nearest relatives she had were her mother's sister and her children as well as the Ngwenya family. She therefore had a semi-orphaned childhood. The absence of siblings and immediate uncles must have had a telling effect on her as she appeared to have somewhat retreated into a shell. While *Amai* obviously cared for her daughter as seen by her taking Rose to Dadaya Mission School where there were better schooling facilities compared to the village school, *Amai's* political activities came between the two and ultimately had a negative effect on their future relationship. On return from Malawi and after a brief stay with *Amai* in Harare, Rose went to work in Bulawayo, thus perpetuating the separation. By the time we got married in 1977, Rose was keen to adopt a new relationship and identity that she hoped would heal her of her past. The fact that she had used four different identities earlier in life compounded matters.

The less than cosy relations between mother and daughter continued until about five or so years prior to Rose's departure when Rose started talking relatively well of *Amai* and providing for her monthly groceries and paying her rentals. We had wanted *Amai* to come and stay in the cottage of our relatively large house but *Amai* preferred otherwise. By the time of her departure, partial rapprochement appears to have been achieved between mother and daughter. Now that Rose is gone, no doubt *Amai* is feeling the void as much as I do. Matters are further compounded by the fact that *Amai* neither fully knew nor understood her only child. Now, any hopes she may have had for complete rapprochement have been shattered. Somehow I have a feeling she thinks I was responsible for the gap that existed between the two of them. Let me take this opportunity to assure her that I was not. Rose was a very single minded person who knew and did what she wanted in life and nothing would take that away from her, not even me. That must have been a result of that childhood background where she had to learn to survive against the odds that would be stacked against her. She was very assertive. The cold relations were there even before I came into her life but matters certainly got worse as she got older and as her values firmed. On the other hand, *Amai's* beliefs had already firmed and thus she remained stuck therein. The polarization that had been latent was concretized.

The matter was compounded by the difference in their approach to life. According to Rose, *Amai's* exposure to nationalist politics and the fact that she has remained unmarried to this day was the major cause of the variance in their characters. It would also appear that Rose failed to forgive or only partially forgave *Amai,* for her being born out of wedlock and that *Amai* stuck to her guns regarding the non-disclosure of Rose's father and his whereabouts. Rose also never approved of some of *Amai's* behavioural patterns. Clearly, these were two very strong characters with neither being prepared to concede to the other…each stuck in her concept of what life ought to be. Ultimately, the only relationship that was there between them was the biological one spiced up with a few flirtations here and there.

The sad thing was that in the process, I also failed to develop a good relationship with *Amai*. Now that Rose is gone, our chances appear to have gone with her. *Amai's* visits to our home were often characterized with long periods of quietness, mainly on Rose's part, which I would occasionally break whenever I felt the silence too heavy to bear. There was rarely any social talk. Rose would also not want *Amai* to visit her place of employment for reasons I cannot state here. Whenever Rose had any misunderstanding with anyone, she always preferred to talk to the person directly and not through a third party (I feel that there should be exceptions to every rule). To this end, I therefore think that had the two parties brought a third party to the equation the misunderstanding could have been somewhat ameliorated. The problem was that this was a cold war, never declared, and therefore no clear disputes and no cause for a ceasefire. Thus there was no victor and no vanquished. As *umkhwenyana*, I could have tried but I never got close enough to *Amai* to gain the confidence to discuss such matters with her. The absence of first generation relatives compounded matters. Thus, this matter appeared to have bothered her from the cradle to the grave (*Yaba yimfinhlo yakhe naphakade*). The full extent of how it bothered her was also her secret until her departure.

This therefore could have been another thorn in Rose's flesh for which she would have prayed for God to deal with. I am reminded of how Paul was in a similar situation and God assured him that his grace was sufficient and that his strength was made perfect in weakness (2 Corinthians 12:7-9).

Reference passages; Gen 33:4, Mat 5:23-26, Luke 23:12

# 7

## Mother and Workhorse

A jack and master of all trades is how I can best describe Rose's industry. There were times when the depth and breadth of what she knew and did as well the level of application left me wondering if she was human. She was simply an enigma.

Whatever she set herself to do and achieve, she did impeccably well. Fellow church members would recall that Rose used to doze a lot during church service and/or evening Bible study. No matter how much I nudged her, it didn't work. At some point, this became a source of great embarrassment for me, until I made an effort to understand the reasons thereof. The answer was very simple; she was always busy, doing one thing or the other and rarely sat down. Even at home, she would doze as soon as she sat on the couch, particularly during the evenings. Many times I would be surprised that I was talking to myself after she had fallen asleep in mid-sentence. The only time Rose would relax would be when she was entertaining a visitor. Even then, she would quickly disappear into the kitchen to prepare an elaborate meal for the visitor, leaving me to entertain the visitor. As soon as the meal was over, she would revert to the couch, dozing. Even though she was a working wife and mother, she always made time to tidy up the house or tend to her plants out in the garden, in addition to other chores, preferring not to fully rely on the domestic workers. There were times when she would wake up around four 4 a.m. or when she would go to bed around midnight…baking and icing cakes or cutting patterns. Although this trend started early in our marriage, it progressed steadily with time until it became an obsession by the time of her departure.

No matter how much I urged her to slow down, she would simply smile it away. Indeed, she appeared to be encouraged to work even harder with me just an observer. She often reminded me of old Boxer in George Orwell's *Animal Farm* who, when reminded of how he was risking his health by always working too hard, would reply, "I will work harder". Hence, she would fall asleep, at times within seconds of touching the couch, as the body would be yearning for rest. The situation got worse during the month prior to her departure as she would hardly sit down and had very little sleep. It would now appear as if something supernatural was telling her that her time was up and thus she was urged to work even harder, this being her 'final lap'. It would appear as if she had to finish her earthly assignments as there would be no one to take over from her once she was gone. In the process, we had very little time together. The memories of seeing her on her favourite couch, facing me, still linger on in my mind and it will take a very long time to erase them. When my *hanzvadzi, Sibonile* Mandizvidza (born Matutu) visited me recently, one of her comments was; "Who is going to doze off on that couch and who is going to cook those nice meals for us now that *Amaiguru* is gone?" Then she started to cry. The combination of a strong and powerful body with a strong willpower as well as a blessed soul was astounding and a rare phenomenon for which I am sincerely grateful to have been associated with. Her 'heart' was certainly not misplaced in that strong body.

Some of the negatives of having a semi-orphaned childhood had already been transformed into positives by the time we got married. Where others would have easily succumbed, she persevered and overcame. **Her strength was in her simplicity.** It has always been clear to me that life had taught her the principles of fearing God, diligence and integrity. These appeared to be her driving virtues for survival. All others were natural fruits of these three. Where others would have spent time mourning about their past, she used that past to shape her future. Consequently, she expected everyone to fit into the same mould and had a problem tolerating otherwise. Also, because of deprivation in earlier life, she dreamt of an idealistic future with a perfect husband and perfect children. She was to be disappointed. Although there was a lot of improvement later in our life, the disappointment lingered on. She must have therefore left this world with her disappointments. Even though she wanted things of quality she did not desire a flashy life. She was not materialistic and was always content with simple things.

Due to her hard working nature, Rose was always a perfectionist. She set extremely high standards in whatever she did. Consequently, she set the same lofty standards for those around her. I would tease her saying that she would never be a successful business person as she would compromise quantity for quality. She would not budge, simply resorted to her trademark smile. **"I would rather celebrate the quality of my work than the quantity of my profit,"** was her firm but humble response at one occasion. I found this approach to be very profound. If only everyone in business was driven by the same values, this world would be a heaven. In today's highly competitive life, the norm is to short change those that we deal with for the sake of profit. Clearly, she was concerned with the welfare of those she dealt with in whatever circumstances. I only fully appreciated this position after her departure when I started looking at her in her totality.

Although she expected me to be like her, I was always clumsy and paid very little attention to detail. Even though this was a point of difference, it never became a source of friction as she always tolerated and accepted me. She never tired of correcting me although there were times when I mistook this for nagging. In fact, she became my tutor in this regard although I did not appreciate it then.

One incident that showed that she always cared for me, even in her sleep, was when at one time I was in serious trouble arising from some allegations that were levelled against me. Whilst both of us were fast asleep, she quickly got up and grabbed me by my wrist. With her big hand, she held me so firmly that I could not wrestle my arm away. We both sat up. I then realized that she was still fast asleep so I had to ensure that she was awake. On enquiry, she explained that she had just rescued me from the edge of a precipice that was so deep I would not have come out if I had fallen therein. She immediately went back to sleep and until the day of her departure, she had no recollection of that incident. The day following this incidence, the allegations that had been hovering over my head were dropped without any explanation.

She was a disciplinarian with regards to children. Whilst I am a bit on the soft side, we always complemented each other on this one. Where I preferred to wait and observe before taking corrective action, she would act immediately. Even though we have always had a house maid and a gardener, she always insisted that the children did their fair share of house chores, especially cooking as well as washing and cleaning up. She would arrange for the maid to go off duty every weekend so that the children would be responsible for their chores. Initially, they resented her style and would rather deal with me. However, I always discouraged them from making a preference between us and supported Rose in her approach. Now that they are grown up, (Lynda is now 22 years old) they fully appreciate the positives of her style, even before she left us. One issue that I never agreed with her was her constant quarrels with Kevin over his mode of dressing which she always took exception to. Kevin preferred to put on an inner shirt with an outer one worn as a jacket with buttons undone. Being bigger than mot boys of his age, he also had to put on large size trousers which looked baggy. I saw nothing wrong with that and tried to reason with Rose to no avail. I also advised her that she risked her long term relationship with Kevin over what I considered to be a trivial matter. I felt that this could have been avoided with a little tolerance on her part. Luckily, at the crucial moment, Kevin left for his studies abroad and the matter never became an issue again.

After losing Rose and on realizing how good she had been to me and how I had disappointed her, a friend reminded me of Genesis 2: 18 where God said, "it is not good for man to live alone; I will make him a helper **comparable** to him". I then wondered as to which one of us was helping the other…for by inference, the helper is expected to contribute less than the principal. But the friend referred to the word "comparable" and reasoned that Rose and I were created specifically to help each other overcome the challenges of this earth and specifically those which God knew we would encounter. Where one was weaker, the other would countermand with his/her strengths. Neither of us would have turned out to be what we became without the other. I indeed thank God that he favoured me to the extent of giving me this angel for a wife. Not so many people have been in this blessed position.

Our relationship was not always cosy. Besides the disappointments that I caused her as mentioned earlier, there were petty differences which I would ascribe to gender differences. While I admit that I was generally reckless and slow in doing things whilst she was cautious and meticulous, she would also cause a storm in a tea cup. In hindsight, it is clear we were focusing on the **minor** differences at the expense of the **major** areas of agreement and complementarity to the detriment of our relationship. We spent energy on the wrong things and were left too weak to focus on relevant areas that would have sustained and made a difference to our relationship. We took each other for granted instead of accommodating and listening to each other. It could have been a case of familiarity breeding contempt, not appreciating what one already has. Clearly, we could have had more quality in our lives.

I am not one who is very particular about my grooming, preferring to put on anything as long as it is not outrageously inappropriate or worn out. Rose was the exact opposite. She would always ensure my clothes were properly washed and ironed. On the occasions when she was available to see me dressing for the office, she would make me change into better clothes as soon as she noticed something amiss. On a number of times she would request me to take off a shirt so that she could either iron it or sew a button on. If my shoes were not properly polished, she would request me to take them off so she could polish them or get someone to do it. Similarly she would often notice my unpolished shoes whilst seated in church and would give me a tissue paper or handkerchief to wipe them. Although I never protested because I knew she meant well, I disliked the taking off of what I had already put on as I felt that she was being petty. She would do the same with the children although in such cases she would instruct the specific child to do whatever was required before leaving for school. They resented that practice.

There was a time when my hair was so long that I was embarrassed. This was not by choice. I had wanted to have it cut but Rose had insisted that I should not go to the public barber shop because I could bring some infection home. I started wondering if having a trained nurse for a wife was an advantage or not. The solution was for me to buy my own set of hair clippers and to this day I cut my own hair and beard. She was also of the view that my head was not round enough for a close shave.

Whilst Rose was always kind and accommodating, she was always firm when it came to her rights as my wife. She would not compromise her feelings whenever she felt I was wrong and she was always blunt in how she put matters across. A good example is how she handled the Kwazi issue (see chapter 4). In this instance, she stood her ground right to the end. The downside of that approach was that she would always assume things, many times wrongly, based on past experience and would therefore prescribe the wrong solutions: a case of wrong medicine for a wrong diagnosis. Naturally, the results would be botched. I have no doubt that she would have been pleasantly surprised had she approached the Kwazi matter from a different perspective.

On the whole, what a pleasant and wonderful wife I had, her weaknesses notwithstanding, for we all have ours. It has been said that a perfect human being has not yet been born and will never be born. If there is a perfect being somewhere, that being is not human. Even the very first person created by God was not perfect. Under such circumstances, give me back my Rose and I will take her back several times over; for she was both mother and wife to me.

Reference passages; Gen 2:18, Gen 18:6, Deut 24:5, Eccl 9: 9-10, 1 Cor 11:11-12 and I Cor 7:14

# 8

# The Housewife

If Rose was kind and generous to my relatives, she exceeded that many times over in her relationship with me. Traditionally, African wives are generally known for their subservience to their husbands. In the early days of our marriage I used to think that she was serving me in pursuant of that tradition and out of duty but I later realized that she did it purely out of love. She would simply go out of her way to please me.

Given her humble background and disposition it was a marvel to note Rose's dexterity and versatility. Our daughter-in-law, Munyaradzi, was to disclose at Rose's funeral that she had been apprehensive to meet Rose after Tatenda had told her that his mother was good at 'everything and anything'. She was therefore not sure of how she would relate and cope with such a mother-in-law. In relative terms, this was not far from the truth. What ever Rose set herself to do; she would do it and perfectly so. She was a perfectionist to a fault.

Rose was simply an enigma. The breadth and depth of the things she could do with her hands and the quality thereof made her a unique personality indeed. On one hand she was a simple and unsophisticated rural woman who could do all the chores expected of a rural woman while on the other hand she had acquired sophisticated skills obtainable from an urban setting. Many a times she would see something unique and beautiful in someone's home or in a shop window and she would set herself to make it, and no matter how long it would take, she would succeed. Where, when and how she had acquired such skills I never knew. She was simply gifted and dedicated. Among many other chores Rose excelled in cooking, baking, gardening, flower arranging, knitting, sewing and singing. I will touch on each of these separately.

## Cooking

Rose had a huge collection of recipes covering soups, sauces, fish, chicken, pork, beef, vegetarian dishes, puddings and cakes among many others. She always made time to cook my favourite dishes like macaroni cheese or grilled tilapia (bream) on a regular basis. She knew my favourite part of the fried bream was the head and would pile these in my plate. She always did things with passion and dedication that I always wondered where she got the time from. She could also make traditional meals she had leant in childhood. These include *nhopi, umxhanxa, umcaba, rupiza, mashakada, mutakura, hodzeko (amase)* and, of course *sadza rezviyo*. After cooking, she would take warm water and towel and kneel for me to wash my hands before bringing the food to me. This always embarrassed me and I always discouraged her from that practice but she would not be persuaded…that was how she preferred to do it. The usual smile would resurface. Although I was uncomfortable with this practice, she had her reasons for it and with time, I let it be. Blending traditional and western cultures has always been a struggle for many, but not with my Rose. She was also very careful with her ingredients as she knew that I do not take spices and acidic foods. When we went for group lunches, she would ensure to prepare my appropriate food or go around tasting the various foods brought by other ladies on my behalf before dishing out. She was my 'official food taster'. Once again, I would be embarrassed.

Apparently, it is the *zviyo/rapoko* porridge, which I take everyday when at home, which has all but cured my stomach acidity condition. I can now take some food substances that I had stopped altogether, like tea and sugar. I strongly recommend it to anyone with a similar problem. Those who have heeded my advice have testified as to its efficacy.

## Baking

She was equally good at baking. She would bake all types of cakes including Christmas, birthday and wedding cakes as well as puddings. My favourite was the carrot cake and pecan nut pie. She also had a passion for cake icing. Budget permitting, we rarely went without a dessert of one kind or another with our meals.

## Gardening

Rose loved various species of plants ranging from the blooming to non blooming types and from seasonal to perennial ones. Once again, it was a puzzle for me as to when and how she learnt the names of all these plants. She would buy all these from various nurseries and would direct the gardener on how and where to plant these. Where the gardener failed to do a good job, she would personally take up pick and shovel, dig the hole and prepare it with compost and plant the plants. Seeing her throw that pick head into the ground was always a marvel to watch and left many men envious. When available, I would obviously do that for her but the point is that she did not depend on someone to do any work for her. It is quite possible that she personally planted seventy five percent of the plants in our front garden. The plants there include cycads, palms, hydrangea, various types of cacti and succulents, yellow lilies, varieties of roses, orchids (at the time of her passing, she had just joined the Zimbabwe Orchids Association), ferns and many others whose names I don't know. Prominent among the roses are the icebergs that line the driveway.

Many other plants are in hanging baskets under the trees while some are in clay pots, both in and outside the house. She also planted fruit trees. I recall one day when I said to her that there is a belief that fruits are rarely eaten by the person who would have planted the tree as such people either die or relocate before the tree starts producing. She laughed and indicated her confidence that we would both eat the fruits. This was not to be, as the unfortunate prophecy was fulfilled. She never ate fruits from the mango, mulberry, guava, avocado and lychee trees, some of which were personally planted by her. As fate would have it, I ate the first mango fruit two months after her departure while the lychee started producing its first flowers six months later. The following season was a major turn around as practically all these trees produced abundantly, as if to spite her.

She had bought a heavy duty cutter with which she would prune the trees and shrubs on a regular basis, a job no ordinary woman would do. The sad thing is that many of the plants which previously struggled to thrive have started to do exceptionally well after her departure, particularly those that she planted in 2007

Taking a stroll in the front garden is always a memory shaker for me and a sad reminder of her industry. Every plant I see invokes fond memories of my dear departed wife and how she would always walk among them whilst talking to each of them as if talking to a person. She had intimate connection to each and every one of those plants as she knew where it had been sourced from, when each was planted and what its specific needs were. For as long as I live on this property, it will be impossible for me to forget that unusual gift of hers as the evidence of her short life will constantly remain before me. Some cacti that she planted shortly before her departure have thrived far much better than the old ones. They just took off like that…as if she is living through them. I have named one which is in my office after her.

## Flower arranging

Some years ago, Rose attended flower arranging classes and would do her own arrangements for both our home and for church service and weddings jointly with Mrs. Alice Mhlanga, a member of the church and wife to Washington, one of the elders at Avondale. As usual, she did that with passion and detail. At times she would make excellent arrangements from dried wild plants and fruits she would have picked on our visits to the village. When on such visits, everyone there would know that *Mai Tatenda* (Tatenda's mother) would be looking for plants, pods and seeds, with the young ones competing on gathering these for her.

## Knitting and crocheting

The only kind of knitting I had known since childhood was that done for me by my mother when I was in boarding school. For a simple uneducated rural woman, she did a good job of it and I was always appreciative of her efforts. Rose brought a new meaning to knitting altogether. The first time I saw her knitting was when Tatenda was born and she did a few booties and complete baby sets for him. All these were manually and painstakingly done. As usual, perfection and quality were the hallmarks of her work. Many ladies who saw these sets would quickly place orders either for their own babies or as gifts. By the time our last child, Lynda, was born, I knew many kinds of wool as she would often send me to buy the wool for her with brief instructions. By then, she had acquired two knitting machines and would knit jerseys for sale. These machines are still around although she had stopped using them for some time. Our extended family and the children were never wanting for jerseys. Rose also crocheted her own table cloths and mats as well as bed spreads among many other items.

She must have learnt her skills from her mother, *uMaNcube* who, in her late seventies, is still very good at knitting.

## Sewing

One would expect the average housewife to have a sound knowledge about sewing. Once again, Rose was no average housewife in this area. She could cut patterns and sew dresses as well as men's shirts with ease. She had a few designs of her own. The crown of her sewing is the various sets of curtains she personally designed and sewed and which are currently hung in the majority of rooms in our home, including the main lounge. Many a lady visitor would marvel at her skills on seeing these curtains and would request that she make some for them although she always declined, on account of the amount of work involved and the painstaking effort and time she always put in such work. On a number of times she would invite my opinion on her handiwork and I would simply commend her for a job well done. I had run out of superlatives and I was afraid that she would think I was flattering her if I continued to say her work was excellent. Simply put, I was dumbfounded and didn't know how to comment although at times she would think I was not appreciative.

## Peanut butter plant

Rose had a small peanut butter making plant comprising a shelling machine, a toaster and a grinding machine. She would drive to the rural areas, at times as far as 200km and waking up as early as 4 a.m. in search of peanuts. With help from one or both of our domestic workers, she would go through all the stages required for making peanut butter. She would then package these for sale. She only stopped this small venture when it became more difficult to source peanuts and when the cost of fuel for the vehicle and other inputs became prohibitive.

This project had somewhat revived my craving for peanut butter. My mother once told me that I liked peanut butter when I was a toddler to the extent she got worried it would have negative effects on my health. Resorting to some advice she had received from friends, one day she prepared a plateful for me in the vain hope that I would get fed up and eventually give up my craving. This failed to achieve the desired results. Her next resort was a similar quantity of the butter with lots of piripiri, a type of hot pepper, sprinkled generously. I ate the butter but started crying. I ate…I cried… I ate…I cried and I ate until the plate was empty. After that I took a well deserved sleep. Needless to say, mother was dumbfounded and simply threw her hands in the air and no further attempts followed. Thereafter, she would always go out of her way to ensure that I had my fair share. I then became so heavy that she struggled to carry me when travelling. My aunties would refuse to carry me. She therefore always left me behind unless she was travelling with father, who would then carry me.

To this day, peanut butter remains one of my favourite foods, plain, spread or cooked. Occasionally, I take it by the tablespoon.

## Singing

Rose was of average talent in singing. She had a sweet and piercing but lovely voice that tended to overshadow those seated next to her. As expected, we would sit together at church services and I had to learn to project my own voice lest I would be overshadowed by hers. Problem was that I have a very discordant voice. Occasionally, Rose would look at me and smile while in the middle of a song and I would straight away know that I had misfired, especially with hymns that needed the baritones or bass to take a lead. I would remind her that not everyone was a good singer and that I was trying my best. I have since taught myself how to avoid the discord and whenever it features, I know how to correct myself. Now I can sing confidently with the knowledge that at least ninety percent of the times I am in sync with the others although the discord has the habit of inviting itself back from time to time. Unfortunately, there will be no one to nudge me or to smile at me when next I misfire.

It would appear she gave up her life so that others, including the plants, would live. I know Rose was not a messiah who would die for others. But by her sheer dedication to the life of others, she gave life to many. In the end, she left us while in the very process of serving others. This is by no means a full list of the things Rose could do, some of which were too intricate for my comprehension. Clearly, I have not done full justice to her talents and industry in this regard.

Reference passages; Prov 31:10-31, Gal 6:10, Matt 20:26, Mark 9:35 and Acts 20:23

# 9

# The Matriarch

Love is all about compromising one's interests for the sake of others, that is the gist of Apostle Paul's teachings in his great lesson on love in 1 Corinthians 13. It was such unconditional love that denominated Rose's outlook to life and I was greatly honoured to have the opportunity to live with such love for a good thirty years.

I mentioned earlier that I am the first born in my family. I am also the first born to my father's generation in our clan. My *sekuru or ubabamkhulu* (paternal grandfather) was the oldest among three brothers and I am the oldest of their generation's grandchildren and the first one to marry. Rose became the first and oldest *muroora* and she acquitted herself very well in that role. She was the mother figure. This role extended to my maternal uncles and their children. She was the most selfless person I have ever had the privilege of knowing.

The Shona language has no equivalent for cousin as one is a *mukoma* (older brother), *munin'gina* (younger brother) or *hanzvadzi* (sister). Similarly, there are no half siblings; a sibling is simply a sibling. Likewise, there are no paternal uncles as they are referred as either *babamunini* (younger father) or *babamukuru* (older father). My father's sister would be my female father (*vatete*), the argument being that if she had been a male, she would have probably been my father. It is even clearer in Ndebele where she is referred to as u*babakazi*. Similarly my mother's sisters are either *amainini*(younger mother) or a*maiguru*(older mother) with their children being my siblings while her brother's children are either *sekuru*(uncle) or a*mainini,* irrespective of age. Married women would address their husbands' relatives exactly the way their children would address them. The rationale is that since children learn to speak from their mothers, (hence the term mother tongue) they must learn the correct terminology at a tender age. Imagine the confusion if the mother would use one term while teaching the child to use a different one for the same person. For example, for Rose to call my brother by his name while teaching Tatenda to call him *babamunini* would be confusing to the young Tatenda. She would therefore simply refer to my younger brother as *babamunini* for the sake of Tatenda. Likewise, Rose would refer to my sister as *vatete.* This background will help the reader to understand the foundation of the Zimbabwean extended family system.

*   *   *

In Zimbabwe and many African customs therefore, it is an accepted and common practice for older siblings to look after the welfare of their younger ones. In fact, society almost demands of it. Being the first born, I had to cut my education prematurely partly due to financial constraints and partly to fend for my *vanin'gina*(younger siblings). When Rose joined me in 1977, I was already staying with three of them, Collet, Lazarus and Philemon. She therefore had little choice but to accept them as part of the family responsibilities. However, at one time the going became tough and Collet had to return to the village as he was already out of school. Imagine a young bride yet to start her own family having to start with a 'ready made one'. The difference came in the way she treated them throughout the period that we stayed with them. She would look after them just as if they were her own children. Philemon, the youngest, was practically like our first born child having started Grade One under our care. By the time the two of them went to secondary school, many people would wonder how we could have such big children when we were relatively young. The clothing and food provisions they took to boarding school made their peers doubt that they were staying with their *Amaiguru*. Many in her position would have behaved otherwise, particularly during the formative stages of our then young family. No doubt, it was not easy and some friction arose occasionally.

\*      \*      \*

Other children from the extended family who stayed with us at one point or another were Athaliah and her sister *Sitembile,* my *vatete's* daughters, who, although their purpose of staying with us was to look after our children, did it with so much distinction that they earned Rose's admiration, because of their integrity and hard work. Rose would always talk about their good behaviour and industry until her departure. It was a feat some of the other children who were to stay with us later failed to achieve.

*Babamunini* Alick, had had his daughter, *Chiedza*, stay with us for two years when studying for her diploma at Harare Polytechnic College.

My *vazukuru*, (sister's children), Sasha and Gracia stayed with us for a number of years each in order to complete their studies. Rose facilitated Sasha's enrolment at a teacher training college where she eventually qualified as a teacher. The two were a mixed bag with one meeting Rose's approval while the other fared very badly. Their mother was later to be added to Rose's medical insurance scheme and by the time she died two months ahead of Rose, the burden of medical bills was not an issue for her. Rose and I met the burial expenses as if it was our direct responsibility with the bulk of the expenses coming direct from her account.

*Simbarashe(Simba)* my brother Smarks' son, had completed four years (Ordinary Level) secondary education at a village school in Gokwe with commendable results but could not proceed due to lack of funds. He had started working for a local cotton company and was contemplating marriage. The possibility of marriage at such a tender age bothered Rose a lot as that would have sealed the end of his educational career. Rose volunteered to take Simba under our wings and sent him to evening school for Advanced Level where he came out with 10 points out of a possible maximum of 15, after studying for only ten months. Suffice it to note that the average child obtains far much lower points after two years' study in a formal school. Rose was vindicated. Simba proved to be a very dependable, hard working and well mannered young man during his stay with us that even the usually strict Rose found no room to complain. She was simply impressed.

When Lazarus and his wife Sandra, who are now based in Australia, suggested that we combine efforts to send Simba for further studies down there, Rose was too pleased to assist. She ran around attending to his papers and contributed significantly to the expenses, including the airfare. Clearly he had won her heart. At the time of writing, Simba had just completed his degree program with double majors in economics and accounting. Well done Simba. Although he had to work double shifts over and above his schooling, and financed the bulk of his university fees, it was the thought and the meeting of initial expenses that made the difference to his life.

During the period Simba was staying with us, *Hlupeko* my other sister's only son also came to stay with us. He opted to train for a diploma in agriculture at a local government college and is now working for the government veterinary department although he remains extremely unhappy with the remuneration in the current highly inflationary environment. He has expressed his desire to also go abroad but our resources have not been very sound lately, what with our own children in university abroad. His mother, *Vongai Nondo*, who is a widow, was diagnosed with high blood pressure in October 2007 during the burial of our sister, Berita. Immediately, Rose added her to her medical insurance scheme as an additional dependent. Once again this was Rose's own initiative and she only told me afterwards. This was yet another demonstration of her unconditional love and willingness to assist a deserving family case.

\*     \*     \*

When my brother, Collet, lost his wife in 2005, Rose and I met the bulk of the funeral expenses. These were mainly the coffin and transport costs from Mutare to Gokwe, a distance of over 700km one way. *Tariro*, Collet's eldest child completed her Advanced Level with good grades in 2006 but could not proceed to university due to lack of funding. When Lazarus and his wife Sandra sent Collet and the children some upkeep money, we realized that it would be enough for Tariro's university fees for one semester at a local church related university and Rose quickly ran around sourcing provisions at her own expense and the two of us took Tariro to Africa University in Mutare. We agreed that between Lazarus and us, we would be able to meet all of Tariro's future university requirements with her father contributing from time to time as his remuneration was too low to meet such expenses. Since that day, Rose had been making efforts to ensure Tariro had adequate money for her meals. Tariro had finally found comfort in her *amaiguru* whom she had taken as a good replacement for her own departed mother. This was not to be. When Collet and his three children visited us on 2 December 2007 supposedly for the December school holidays, they had no idea that they were coming for a big 'farewell'. Subsequently, they never returned to Mutare following Collet's transfer to Harare at about the same time. Naturally, they played a very important role in keeping me company during the healing process after everyone else had gone back to their bases. I managed to get places for them at local schools.

Lazarus and Sandra have since kindly facilitated Tariro's move to an Australian university where she has already started her studies.

\* \* \*

My late father, *Mhembedzo* Peter Matutu, was an age mate with his *babamunini's* son, *Nkosana*. In our tradition the two were therefore brothers. Nkosana is also my 'father' and many people do not know that he is not my real father. Nkosana's son, Solomon, was like a blood brother to me, and many people believed it to be so. When Solomon died in Harare in the year 2000, Rose suggested that he be mourned at our place for the convenience of mourners as he stayed at a government college 200 kilometres out of Harare and had no house of his own in Harare. Further, it would be convenient for his father and uncles who would come from Zambia where they are based. In later years, Solomon's daughter, *Kudakwashe* Samantha, would stay with us in order for her to pursue her studies, once again, courtesy of Rose's generosity. She moved out when she got a job with a local bank.

\* \* \*

The only person we stayed with us from Rose's side of the family was Maurice Ngole, son to *sekuru* Henry. Maurice left after a brief stay as he and Rose did not get along well at some point. We also had occasion to assist Castro Ngole, Maurice's brother, with his Advanced Level examination fees. Castro had always been extremely good in school but had opted for employment before he did Ordinary Level which he later did by private study and acquitted himself very well. Besides the occasional gifts for *sekuru* Ngole and his wife as well as for Rose's cousins, not much else was done for her side of the family. I have no doubt that more would have been done had her family background been different.

This is by no means the full list of children who stayed with us over the 30 years of our marriage. Obviously there were misunderstandings here and there with either these children or with their parents, for Rose was always a disciplinarian and would not tolerate laziness, a trait which others mistook for cruelty. Despite these misunderstandings, Rose would not be negatively influenced against taking the next child by the behaviour of the other. No doubt, we were not able to accommodate everyone who would have wanted to stay with us due to various constraints.

\*    \*    \*

In secular life and today's cut throat corporate competitiveness, humility is variably taken for docility and complicity. Despite her position as the mother of the clan, she never claimed that position either formally or by deed. She maintained her humility whatever the circumstances, content with giving the occasional guidance. In many families, it is the right of a person in her position to instruct, supervise and delegate work from a distance, especially at family gatherings. Not so with my Rose. She would be leading from the front like a gallant general of old, even in the hottest sun. Instead, it was the junior *varoora* who would need to be dragged to the fire place. She also had a back problem like me but would prefer to complain about it later in the evening when we retire to bed. No matter how much I tried to make her see things differently, she would simply not budge, preferring to do things her way. She would just smile at me.

*   *   *

The first people to be added to Rose's medical aid outside our nucleus family were our two mothers. When my mother, who was diabetic, became critically ill, she came under our direct care, both at home and in hospital. On the occasions she was discharged from hospital, Rose would personally and physically wash my mother's sores to the amazement of many who could not understand how a *muroora* would do that for her mother-in-law. This is taboo in Zimbabwean African custom. Despite the torment my mother went through during her final days, which made her very temperamental, she died fully appreciative of my wife's love and commitment for her. At intervals and on separate occasions, my two grandmothers would also visit us on invitation and both were fairly advanced in age. My wife would personally take warm water, soap and towel and wash their feet and apply ointment…and give them warm blankets for their feet, all to their amazement. Even from the world of the dead, my grandmothers and mother appear to be appreciative of Rose's love for them. I was therefore overwhelmed when these three ladies appeared to me in a dream a few days before Rose's accident, as if to herald the news or to welcome her into their world (please refer to chapter 16). They appeared to have fully accepted her into the family, even in death.

*   *   *

A cousin of mine, *mukoma* Samuel Moyo, died about ten years ago leaving behind a wife and children. In 2006, his wife had a stroke that left her partially paralyzed. At one time Rose adopted a punishing schedule for herself in order to help Mrs. Moyo. Rose would leave work at 17:00hrs and dash to pick her up for some physiotherapy at our home then return her home before going for her group study sessions. Rose simply went out of her way to assist despite the punishing routine. Unfortunately, there was not much progress as the sessions were discontinued at some point at the patient's initiative. Mrs. Moyo passed away eight months after Rose left us.

\*     \*     \*

Over the years, many other relatives of mine would visit us for one reason or the other and Rose would be generous to all of them alike. I mentioned earlier that she did not have many relatives of her own, and that mine became hers. Some of these relatives of mine would reciprocate the generosity while others would not, preferring to take her for granted, but Rose did not discriminate even though some went to the extent of stealing some items like utensils and linen from our home on their regular visits. Although she would have her suspects it would take a lot of effort on my part for her to open up on such issues and mention them. Nonetheless, there were times when she preferred to ignore such issues. In such instances she would strongly protest whenever I indicated my intentions to confront the individuals concerned. At times I had a feeling that her desire not to rock the boat was in self interest as she would not like to antagonize any relationships. By saying this, I do not mean to take anything away from her. Whatever the motive, she acquitted herself so well that even her detractors were always amazed and disarmed.

\*     \*     \*

Rose was a member of the benevolence ministry at church and at first I thought she had joined that particular ministry by default as she could have joined any other. But once again, despite her punishing schedule, she would always join other members of the ministry whenever they went on an outreach visit outside town to donate some goods. She would volunteer to source scarce commodities for the needy, a not so easy task in our current economic environment which is characterized by a severe shortage of commodities. It was the zeal with which she did it that made the difference. Rose was the secretary of this ministry. The ministry's office bearers were supposed to change annually but she served happily in that capacity for five years until her departure as others who were nominated to succeed her always turned down such nominations.

*   *   *

Whenever we were visited by any of our relatives or when we visited them, Rose would go out of her way to get them some groceries and vegetables. Throughout her life, when Rose decided to give, she did so without measurement. She would just give, abundantly. She only used measurements in her work such as baking and sewing, not when giving. She would share with anyone, whether that person was well to do or not. **She did not give in anticipation of receiving in turn.** While Rose was very keen on her flower garden, she showed very limited interest in our thriving vegetable garden, which was my forte. Interestingly when the vegetables were ready for marketing, she would be the first one to harvest for her friends who all knew her for her generosity. I often expressed my displeasure with her on the extent of her generosity, especially considering that most of these vegetables were grown for commercial purposes. On that matter, she was as stubborn as they come; she would simply ignore me and once again give her trademark smile. There were times when she felt slighted when I discouraged her from giving abundantly. Her urge for giving was simply insatiable.

Although I have always found pleasure in sharing with my loved ones, I learnt new heights of giving from Rose. Her motto was that whenever we have been blessed with material possessions, no matter how much or little, we should always think of others, both the fortunate and less fortunate.

\*       \*       \*

Let me share my thoughts on giving. Giving must be done without an anticipation of receiving in turn otherwise the giving is in vain. However, giving must not be limited to material items only, but should apply to love and time as well. That way, giving should not hurt but should be pleasurable and rewarding as it should come from the heart. However, I have two principles that have guided my giving all my life which I need to share. I only give when two fundamental conditions have been met. First and foremost, the **will** to give, either voluntarily or after a request, must be there. The desire to give should be from within. Compelled giving is anything but giving. Secondly, I must **afford** the gift. Giving without affordability may result in giving what belongs to others, and is therefore not giving. Thus, when these conditions are met, I will not have any regrets. I also never give solely because someone expects me to give or because I want to be appreciated; otherwise I will be disappointed when the other person fails to appreciate. However, it is always a bonus to be appreciated; one is encouraged to give more. However, that should not be the motivation. I have witnessed cases where a beneficiary has complained that he/she has been given too little or simply does not acknowledge the gift. Whilst this may discourage the giver, one should never stop giving with the full knowledge that this is part of our humble service to our Lord.

I also enjoy, to very significant degree, sharing (consuming) whatever I may have with those I love. I see no value in, for example, having a nice meal by myself. That meal will be far much nicer with a loved one around. With my partner now gone, I struggle a lot on this front.

\*     \*     \*

There was a lady whom I shall simply call Lady X who, although a lot younger, had grown up in the same village as Rose. When Lady X completed her secondary education she came to Harare for her technical training and stayed with Rose's mother for a number of years. After some years in government service she left to join the private sector. It so happened that Rose also joined the same organization and was junior to Lady X. Whenever internal vacancies arose for which Rose qualified, we would discuss her options and many times we would agree that she needed to apply. Regrettably, on a number of occasions, she was unsuccessful and she was convinced that Lady X had influenced the outcome as somehow, Lady X had developed a very negative and patronizing attitude towards both of us. At first I did not believe her but she justified her reasoning. It got to a stage where it affected the quality of our life as Rose would come home so despondent that she would talk about the issue until very late at night, at times crying. This left me frustrated and helpless as I failed to help my wife in her hour of need. It is simply for this reason that I recount this issue here otherwise there is no reward arising from issues that may be on the subjective side.

On one occasion we visited Lady X's parents in the village and I intended to talk to her father on the matter on a man to man basis. Rose was against the idea. It turned out that he was not home on that day. I expressed my desire to talk to him but his wife suggested that I discuss whatever issues I had with her but I declined. It had been rumoured that Lady X's mother had expressed her displeasure as soon as Rose joined this company as she felt Rose was competing with her daughter in what she considered to be a very well paying job. A few months later, another vacancy arose and I persuaded Rose to apply against her wish. Then a sudden change occurred. Lady X encouraged her to apply and Rose wondered why the sudden change of heart. Rose was eventually successful. To us, the influence of Lady X in the outcome was clearly evident.

All was well and good up to this stage. When, a few months later, we met Lady X's mother, to our amazement her greeting words were; "Congratulations, the problem is now over." When I enquired from her what problem she was referring to, she quickly changed the subject upon realizing that she would expose herself further. Neither of us had ever mentioned any problem to her and had not told her of the successful application. My conclusion was that our earlier fears of Lady X's negative influence had been vindicated and that my earlier interest to talk with her father had warned them that we were aware of her schemes.

Lady X died ahead of Rose and Rose went to her funeral. Lady X's mother unreservedly expressed her appreciation for Rose's attitude without any elaboration. I did not feel comfortable to go to the funeral as I was still bitter then. Please note here that Rose, the real offended party, was so forgiving compared to me, a third party.

$$* \quad * \quad *$$

Although it takes a lot of provocation for me to be offended, I have always struggled in forgiving those who hurt me once I have drawn the line. Failure to forgive compromises the quality of life of both the offender and the offended as both are consumed by hatred in the process. Unnecessary expenditure of energy and material resources is oft incurred in pursuit of revenge to no avail while forgiving restores the status ante. This was a major lesson for me from my dear wife. I felt ashamed of myself. She indeed was a giant of a character.

*   *   *

Rose was always very courteous, to a fault. At times I found her too courteous I would be embarrassed. In Zimbabwean culture, it is always the younger or junior person who should ask after the health of the older ones after the initial exchanging of greetings. It is a sign of respect for the elderly when the younger or junior person takes the initiative. This is one aspect of our culture Rose never related to and completely ignored. She was always the more courteous and would ask after the health of anyone despite their seniority or station in life, even children. It was not as if she did not know of the practice, it was simply immaterial to her. I always reminded her of the protocol but as usual, she ignored me. Whilst this may appear immaterial in western cultures, it is a major issue in Zimbabwe, especially among the Shona people.

Maintaining traditional cultures gives a people some identity. While some traditional practices have proved harmful to the modern generation, others have proved useful while yet others are simply irrelevant and redundant. Clearly, the harmful and redundant ones should be discarded while the others can be tolerated. However, keeping them for the sake of complying can be counter productive and harmful to both body and soul.

*   *   *

I have no doubt whatsoever that Rose appreciated me as an individual, as her husband as well as in the context of the extended family. What I may be uncertain of is why she went out of her way to provide for my extended family. Was it reciprocation in turn? In the unlikely event that she did not appreciate me, did she do it notwithstanding her disapproval? Whichever way one looks at it, many in her position would have failed dismally to rise to the occasion. Indeed, even after reading this book, many will still fail; not that they are necessarily obliged to.

*     *     *

As can be seen, Rose was indeed a special being, not only to me and my relatives but to many others who had the privilege of knowing or meeting her. I am reminded of one testimony I heard from a lady that I had never met. She recounted how she had met Rose who, on realizing the need that she was in, went to Mbare Musika (market place) where she bought a lot of vegetables which together with some groceries were delivered to this lady's home. As she recounted this incident, this lady was in tears. I listened with disbelief as Rose had never mentioned this incident to me. I only believed when Mrs. Maraura, Tatenda's mother-in-law confirmed it. There were a couple of other similar testimonies from both acquaintances and strangers that together left me dumbfounded. 'Is this the same person with whom I lived for 30 years, whom I am only discovering now, after her departure? God forgive me, for I am indeed a sinner.'

**Hers was a life of service and leading by example, in season and out of season (2 Tim 4:2).** I am more than confident that I have in no way exaggerated her skills in the previous chapter and her charity in this one. If anything, I could have done an injustice. She amply demonstrated, literally, the meaning of the maxim "charity begins at home". Many with childhoods similar to hers would have been bitter with life and would have refused to give their best back to that very life. Although Rose appeared to have been adversely affected as reflected in Chapter 6, on the whole, she acquitted herself commendably.

Now that I have been left alone, I doubt that I will be able to play my patriarchal role as well as I did with Rose's support and encouragement. I would also like to urge my extended family not to expect anyone I may get married to in future, God willing, to be a replica of Rose as every person is unique. I also believe that a marriage union is a gift from God and like any other, it comes at a given time in someone's life and for a given purpose, uniquely packaged. Should my next gift be a multiple or a fraction of my earlier portion, I will accept it graciously. Only God will know why it would be so. What is definite is that it will not be a replica, except through a miracle.

Reference passages;

1. Kings 3:7, Matt 18:2-4, Matt 20:26, Eph 3:18, John 13:14-16,
2. Matt 5: 42, 1 John 3: 17-18, 1 Tim 6;18-19, Rom 12:8, Acts 20:35, 1 Cor 13:1-3, Gal 6:9,
3. Psalm 94:1, Mark 11:25, Matt 18 21-22, Rom 9:14, Rom 12: 14-21, Rom 12:19, Gal 1:14, Col 3:13, 1 Pet 3;19,

# 10

# The Employee

Due to the nature of my job in the banking industry I was frequently transferred from one town to another in Zimbabwe and at one time I was moved to Nairobi, Kenya, for two years. Accordingly, Rose and the children always followed me wherever I went. She was therefore forced to change employers at the frequency of my transfers and on some occasions, she failed to get employment at our new destination. Some of the employers and places she worked for are Marondera Polyclinic in Bulawayo, Bulawayo City Council's Njube and Pelandaba clinics, as well as Gwanda, Marondera, Kwekwe, Rusape and Chitungwiza General Hospitals.

The only employer whom she served for what I would consider a reasonable period of time was the Premier Services Medical Aid Society (PSMAS) for whom she worked in excess of ten years. I have therefore included herein a testimony from this employer, with their consent, which I think is representative of all the other employers.

## Work history

Rose joined PSMAS on 01/04/1996. She was promoted to position of senior assessor on 01/10/2003.

On 1/02/2005 she was promoted to claims supervisor, a position which she held until her death. I worked with her as a fellow assessor and later as her immediate superior from the time she was promoted.

## Work Performance

Rose was a diligent worker who was always very thorough and organized. Rose's work station was always orderly and tidy; she was always smart.

She was always helpful to all her colleagues and had no prejudices. A colleague narrated how she was taught of letter writing skills by Rose. In her own words she says; "Rose was particularly organized, neat and thorough in whatever she set herself to do".

Rose interacted professionally with the Society's members, our clients. She had a unique approach to life which enabled her to handle even the most difficult of our members with tact. She received a number of letters praising her for excellent service which are still in her file to this day.

Part of her duties as senior assessor involved dealing with external service providers including doctors and hospitals who all respected her for her maturity and quality of service delivery. In some instances, third parties preferred to deal with Rose on matters not related to her department because of the quality of her service.

As a supervisor Rose showed her capabilities in leading a team of fourteen subordinates. This team was the first to process claims electronically at PSMAS. She met the challenges that come with any new project head on .True to her character she worked well with all *people involved. She paid attention to detail and her thoroughness is evident in the systems that she set up which are still functional and relevant to this day. Thanks to her untiring efforts the work processes are now flowing smoothly. We now have a challenge in having these maintained.*

*In meetings Rose would stand her ground to push a point home without necessarily causing friction. This earned her the respect of her colleagues.*

### <u>Rose the person</u>

*I got to know Rose the person over the years. She had a passion for flowers and her office always had a thriving plant of one kind or another. She absolutely loved orchids which when in bloom, she would have one in her office. If one had a sickly plant in one's office one could always trust Rose to volunteer advice on how to revive it.*

*Rose was health conscious. She was particular about the food she ate and how it was prepared. If ever in doubt, she would rather not eat. She swore by the good effect calcium supplements had had on her osteoporosis and encouraged all the ladies to take the same as a preventative measure.*

*Rose was very, very smart and hygiene conscious. I would often tease her on noticing how she would scrub a mango at the canteen sink using dishwashing liquid. She would never eat any fruit, including the ones with peels, without washing it first.*

*Although she was smart she was not vain. I know she kept a mirror next to her computer, because as she used to say, one has to look presentable when dealing with the public. She used to say one can be smiling at a member with something unsightly on one's face or teeth. That is how that mirror became a permanent feature on her desk.*

*And oh that smile! Rose was always smiling; she always had a sweet spirit about her. One would always feel encouraged after an encounter with her.*

*We were honoured to attend her son's wedding in 2006. Rose was just glowing with excitement and happiness on that day. After the wedding she talked about how proud Tatenda had made her.*

*In Rose, the saying "action speaks louder than words" rang true. She was a doer and not a talker; she walked the talk. Her actions showed how much she cared for people around her. She was a giver. Colleagues testify to receiving produce from her garden for free. She was always thoughtful, and would remember to advise her colleagues whenever she came across items in short supply. Many times she would just buy for her colleagues and recover her money later.*

*She would offer transport to others in order to attend weddings and funerals as well as visiting the sick in hospital.*

*We were indeed very blessed and privileged to have been a part of Rose s life. She has indeed left an indelible mark at PSMAS. We all sorely miss her.*

*May her dear soul rest in peace!*

# 11

# Fruits of the Spirit

While Rose was not in any way perfect, for no one is perfect, it is clear from the earlier chapters that she was a unique person. I do not wish to credit Rose the person with these good works and attributes, for none of us by ourselves are capable of attaining such levels of commitment without the guidance of the Holy Spirit.

When writing to the Christians of Galatia, Paul made reference to the fruits of the Spirit which are, "love, joy, peace, longsuffering, kindness, goodness, faithfulness, gentleness and self control", see Galatians 5:22, 23".

Of the nine virtues I fail to identify the one least applicable to Rose. Many a times I would marvel at how she would restrain me from doing something I would have considered normal only to reflect later and see that she was right after all. Earlier in our marriage, I would think that she was putting on a mask for the benefit of third parties but with time I realized she was very genuine in whatever she did. What was peculiar was that until as recently as four years ago, she was not a regular reader of the Bible yet these virtues came out of her almost naturally. She did not need to put much effort for third parties to realize that she was unique.

My Bible quotes the definition of kindness from Strong as; *goodness in action, sweetness of disposition, gentleness in dealing with others, benevolence, affability, …the ability to act for the welfare of those taxing one's patience and lack of abrasiveness.* I find these definitions to be inclusive of all the other virtues mentioned by Apostle Paul as well. I am sure those who knew Rose would find it difficult to find one definition out of these which did not apply to her fully. Would it therefore be amiss for me to refer to her as an 'angel' seeing that not many people I know would be so disposed? Where else could she have got them from except directly from God? I am aware that there have been, that there are and that there shall always be, individuals far much better than Rose in many respects, for she was not the epitome of God's creation… only that I was privileged to be part of her life.

In 1 Corinthians15:10, Paul writes; "By the grace of God I am what I am and his grace, which was bestowed upon me was not in vain; but I laboured more abundantly than they all **yet not I but the grace of God which was within me**"( my emphasis). Clearly, Rose had an abundance of God's grace thrust upon her and she does not appear to have disappointed her maker until the end. What ever she did, she did out of God's grace and not out her effort or ingenuity.

Where Rose lacked in literary knowledge, she excelled in the application of her spiritual obligations, thanks to the Holy Spirit that dwelt within her. Where tuition fell short, intuition prevailed.

# 12

## Disparate Dispositions

No two individuals are identical, neither in form nor in substance. This is more so between strangers, for in a majority of cases it is strangers who marry. Expecting them to see and do things the same way will therefore be expecting the impossible. It is how these two individual reconcile their differences that matters and God gave us the marriage union as one of the vehicles by which these may be overcome. It is never plain sailing but hard work. We should remember however, that marriage is different from all other unions, it is a holy union. That should make the difference. The level of compromise must therefore be higher than in any other union...but as humans, we always struggle.

While Rose and I had a lot in common which bonded us together, there were areas where our dispositions were divergent and at times clashing. This is to be expected from any married couple as our dispositions are influenced by different factors encompassing genetic, hormonal and social among many others. The mere fact that one is female while the other is male is a major source of differences. Such differences should therefore be taken as a norm rather than an exception. In our case, this called for a lot of tolerance and accommodation for each other and I am glad that in the final analysis, we managed to overcome most of our differences. This was not an easy task by any definition. By including this chapter and the next, I am neither criticizing Rose nor am I claiming to have been better than her. I am simply acknowledging the differences and how they impacted on our lives. Please bear with me if it comes out otherwise.

*    *    *

Rose did not have much sense of humour or fun. This was a major contradiction between us which caused unnecessary friction on a number of times. I always look at the brighter side of things and enjoy my fun while she was always serious with life. There were times when she would think I was laughing at her if my joke was directed at her or if I just found her actions funny. On the other hand, she could criticize me as bluntly as she possibly could although with time, restraint crept in. I had to learn to suppress my urge for jokes for her sake when I felt that she would possibly take it negatively. She would also express her disquiet at some of my jokes in the presence of third parties, concerned that the jokes could be misunderstood or would reflect me or both of us in bad light. As a result, there were times when we were deprived of what could have been good fun. I have always wondered if my jokes are that bad although I do admit that there were occasions when some of them were inappropriate. In what appears to be a contradiction, she was always in a joyous mood coupled with that infectious laugh, as if to say; "Let's be happy but no jokes please."

That is not to say we never had fun together, we had lots of it throughout our life together but we could have had more. I remember one incident which she always recounted with uncontrollable laughter. I had told her of my experience when

I stayed in a four star hotel for the first time, at my employer's expense. With my strong rural background and coming from a poor family, I had very little sense for quality and good standards. After spending my very first night in the hotel, I left my face towel to dry in the bathroom. When I returned in the evening, I couldn't find my towel and enquired from the house keeper if anyone had seen it. The answer was in the negative. When I insisted that I had definitely left my towel which was now missing, the lady on the other end of the phone politely told me that what she had seen was a very dirty and torn rug which she had thrown away. To say that I was embarrassed is a gross understatement. It was as if the whole world was listening in.

Another incident that she would not forget was when I was working for a tyre manufacturing factory in Bulawayo as a finished goods inspector. One cold winter night, I was on a twelve hour night shift when work became a bit slack and I decided to take a nap. I neatly rolled myself up inside a size 32 rear tractor tyre, still warm from the press. Although this was not the first time I had done it, I must have overslept that night and was caught at it by the night supervisor. Needless to say, that is how I lost my first substantive job.

*       *       *

As someone who grew up in a wooded and mountainous countryside, I have always loved the wild, both flora and fauna. On a number of times we visited similar areas of interest but I would notice Rose would not be as excited as I would be. For the two years that we stayed in Kenya we visited many tourist areas including the Rift Valley lakes of Naivasha and Nakuru, Amboseli National Park on the foothills of Mt. Kilimanjaro, Ngoro Ngoro Crater in Tanzania, Mt. Kenya, Diani Beach in Mombasa south coast, Malindi and Magadi salt lake among others. Here in

Zimbabwe we have visited Victoria Falls, Nyanga Mountains, Bvumba and house boats on Lake Kariba several times. Any ordinary person would be excited visiting such places but Rose's excitement was always muted. I had hoped that Diani Beach would be different, what with lots of coconuts and sea fish as well as sun bathing on those beautiful white sands. She would always carry her seriousness of life with her although one would notice some sparks of excitement from time to time. Conjugal activity was almost always not for consideration once she suspected the hygiene of a given holiday resort or facility. I always struggled with that as it took away the fun from the holiday.

On some occasions we had to cancel travel arrangements when she insisted there was no value to be derived from the holiday particularly when we had previously visited the intended destination. Give me a houseboat trip on Lake Kariba every year and I will grab it while Rose would decline on the basis that the weather in Kariba is too hot, yet that change is the source of the fun. On the few occasions that we went down there, Rose was always miserable, with the odd moments of excitement.

\*   \*   \*

Both of us were of quiet and reserved dispositions and not very outgoing in our youth, as has been mentioned earlier. Although we have both remained introverts in adult life, my drinking days and exposure at work brought some slight change in me. However, Rose maintained her original disposition to a large extent. We were later to struggle in our marriage as her style somewhat dominated mine to the extent that we had very little social life. Rose was of the view that one cannot visit without an invitation. Even when invited, she would expect a certain type of decorum from me and the children to the extent that one was somewhat restricted and the whole purpose of friendship would be defeated.

In the process we lost out on many potential friendships. When entertaining visitors, Rose always went out of her way to cook very expensive and elaborate meals; usually three course meals. This entailed a lot of work and cost, and being the thorough person that she was, there were no short cuts. Entertaining visitors was therefore synonymous with lots of work and this made her and the children dislike entertaining. It became a deterrent. My advices that simple and common meals that we often had as a family would also suffice for visitors were rarely taken. On the odd occasion she took the advice, she would be pleasantly surprised at the outcome. Thus, outside of workmates and church mates, we had very few friends and it has always been my view that this was wrong but I couldn't move her, being the strong personality that she was. And as is known, in many cases workmates are just that, mates while working together. She however had a few really good friends from her work place.

There was one couple with whom we could have been very good friends as the ladies got along very well. Somehow the men did not click that much despite that we had known each other before both of us got married. I think it had something to do with the fact that when the other gentleman's father died some years ago, I was too young and immature to go and pay my condolences. I simply did not know what I was supposed to do when I got there as I had never been among mourners. So, I simply did not go. I was later to regret this as I became more mature and saw the need to console one another in times of bereavement but it was too late to correct the omission. When Rose passed on, the couple did not say a word of condolence, even over the phone, even though they had received the news. I certainly have no hard feelings but I was just surprised that they could keep a 'grudge' for so long.

There were many other couples with whom we failed to cultivate good friendships despite a lot of goodwill between us.

*    *    *

Being the strong character that she was and with little room for compromise, Rose would shut me out without talking to me for days on end whenever I offended her; what some people would call 'the silent treatment'. Talking would be restricted to *mangwanani, masikati* and *manheru* and perhaps, a few questions when it became very necessary. I have heard that this is a fairly common practice in many households in Zimbabwe. I could just not stand this 'treatment' and would go out of my way to persuade her to talk. She would only resume talking to me when she felt matters had improved or whenever we received a respected visitor. Meanwhile, she would perform all her chores as usual although subdued at times. The bedroom always suffered in such cases. Although in some instances I would have offended her, in many instances I would not have wronged her at all but she would be basing her position on either assumption or misunderstanding. There were times when I considered apologizing even when I was in the right, just to achieve peace.

Granted, this is a cowardly way of solving disputes but I always struggled with this approach of hers to solving issues. Admittedly, I was a bit of a weakling. At times I suspected that she was taking advantage of me as she knew I could not handle these silent treatments well and always ended up begging her for an opportunity to make it up to her. However, I later realized that she would have based her conclusions on past experiences where in some cases, I would have wronged her. **It was a matter of trust which, when lost once, would be very difficult to regain.** By default I was therefore clearly the offender in many of these cases.

*    *    *

As has already been mentioned, I was prone to being unfaithful to my marriage vows in our earlier days whereas I am convinced that she remained faithful until death did us part. This was by far the single biggest difference we had and which had the most negative effect on our relationship. We had to live with these effects for the entire subsistence of our marriage and the quality thereof was obviously adversely affected. What could have been an excellent marriage ended up being just an ordinary one. In her magnanimity, she forgave me although she would not forget, resorting to the once bitten twice shy concept. It would have been unfair for me to expect her to do otherwise.

\*     \*     \*

On a number of times when I went abroad on business I would find myself buying some goods for Rose and the children and very little or nothing for myself. This was never by design. Although she always acknowledged this disparity, she did not appear to appreciate the gesture until on one occasion when she said; "It is not that I do not appreciate what you do for me, I do. However, I appreciate your love more than I do these gifts, as presents given without love are meaningless to me." It was not as if I was covering up anything with these gifts. I simply enjoy giving to those close to me and that is why I am prepared to deprive myself.

\*     \*     \*

Whereas Rose was always serious about life, I often took a lackadaisical approach to things. On many occasions she would ask me to do something, either personally for her or for the family, and it would take me a number of reminders and at times remonstrations, before I could do it. I tended to procrastinate. However, I always attended to major issues with urgency whereas to her everything was major, hence the difference of approach. I would always wonder what the fuss would have been all about.

*   *   *

Having said all this, I know that we had our share of high and low moments, our happy and sad ones, the sweet and the sour, dark moments and light ones, but when I look back I can only see the highs, the light and happy moments…the sweet and the positives… for the lows and sad and all the negatives have gone. Such negatives cannot live in the vacuum that has been created by Rose's departure. It is the positives that will see me through whatever remains of my life; the positives that she has left behind for my sustenance. Indeed, I will cherish them for the rest of my life for nothing will ever take that away from me.

In retrospect, I have learnt that failure to appreciate how my partner viewed and valued certain issues was a reflection of a lack of concern and interest on my part and was a major contributor to the disharmony in our home. I should have made positive note of the 'little' concerns that she raised and to appreciate the things that she had interest in and those that made her tick. The little concerns have a habit of becoming giant monsters when left unattended. I am guilty of classifying almost everything as nagging when in actual fact it was expression of concern and love. The best that we can do is to accept that there will always be differences between how men and women look at issues. That will help us to adjust in a spirit of give and take…for without that, no marriage can last.

# 13

# Her Weaknesses

The tough are not only expected to make bold decisions but also to have the courage to reverse such decisions when circumstances dictate so. Where such a reversal is deemed too late to prevent undesired consequences, then one should accept such consequences gracefully. The ability to compromise is therefore an essential part of decision making. Rigidity can only be counterproductive. Failure to flex is a recipe for breakage.

It would be amiss for me to write about Rose's good side while ignoring her weaknesses. She had her fair share of these, just like all of us... for no one is perfect, not even one. Even as I look at these weaknesses, my assessment of such weaknesses is obviously subjective, coming from a mortal being like me. It is therefore not my intention, whatsoever, to judge but to present Rose in the context of her relationship with me.

As mentioned earlier, one of her shortcomings was her failure to compromise with those who failed to measure up to her values and virtues of hard work and integrity. If one disappointed her once, it would take special effort on the part of the offender to be appreciated by her again. However, once she trusted someone, she would go out of her way to accommodate that person.

Being the perfectionist that she was, Rose expected everybody else to be like her. She could just not understand how others were so different yet that is the nature of mankind. There are so many forces at play in the formulation of our personalities that no two people are the same. Consequently, she always took a knock whenever someone let her down. Without being hard on her, I would tell her that she was rather naïve to expect everyone to meet her standard. She expected the world to be perfect without realizing that her view of that world was not necessarily the most vantage and spectacular one.

Because Rose was always given to perfection, she struggled whenever I disappointed her. On one hand she would be angry with me while on the other she would not want the world to know. "Why wash our dirty linen in public?" she would ask. She would also try hard to hide the situation from the children although they could always tell there was something wrong between us. The children were to remark on this issue after her departure when they told me that they had always thought that we were a perfect couple and that they had boasted about it to their friends. However, their friends had cautioned them, saying that there was nothing like a perfect couple. The children felt that they deserved to have known the truth. "It is as if you lived a lie," one of them said. They have however appreciated this position in hindsight as they realise that they were being protected from situations that could have traumatized them.

*     *     *

The weakness that I struggled with most was her failure to accept correction when, in my view, she would be wrong or had made a mistake. She always took correction for negative criticism or condemnation, no matter how well put or intended. She simply took offence and would resort to the 'silent treatment'. I would try to reason with her to no avail as she would also take that as criticism. The downside to this was that we failed to correct certain things in good time to our detriment as a family unit. By contrast, she was quick to correct me no matter how small the need for correction. I had to rationalise that it as her nature. It has also been my observation that this problem was not unique to us; it appears to be common in many families and I would like to think that there are families out there who can identify with this problem. Regrettably, my daughter, Lynda, appears to have inherited this trait from her mum and by mentioning it here, I hope she will not take it as negative criticism and that it will help her as a constant reminder whenever this manifests itself. Meanwhile, I have discussed the matter with Lynda who has agreed to work on the problem. However, she explains that she often withdraws not because she cannot accept criticism, but because she will be remorseful. I would like to think that it is both. No one is infallible, even angels have erred.

\*     \*     \*

Rose always forgave her offenders but would rarely forget. I would be surprised when she would bring up something I would have done long back but which I would have completely forgotten about. I often wondered if this was in fulfilment of the Shona proverb; *chinokanganwa idemo asi muti haukanganwi pawakambotemwa*. Literally translated, this means that it is the axe that always forgets that it once cut a tree but the tree never forgets as it struggles to mend its wounds. Many times I wondered if it was a conscious case of 'I will forgive but will not forget' or whether it just happened naturally. I cannot pretend that these issues did not bother me, they did, but I always took comfort in that her balance sheet portrayed a massive net positive position which she eventually took with her to the yonder world.

*   *   *

I have referred to Rose's semi orphaned background and that she grew up with many girls of her age. Although I am sure *Amai* always provided for her needs, our African culture demands that we share whatever we have with those without. Rose would therefore share blankets with her peers, a situation which demanded that she had to become hardened in order to survive. During the cold winters one would therefore need to ensure that the blankets are not pulled away by one's sleeping partner by tucking them firmly on one's side. This can only be the explanation when this tendency became evident in our marriage as she would often tuck the blankets on her side of the bed, when there would be clearly no need for that, and I would have to wake her up so that she could release the blankets for me. Although she would feel embarrassed and always apologized, there was nothing she could do about it because it would have been by natural reflex as soon as she felt the cold.

*   *   *

On my part, I became a heavy snorer as soon as I turned forty, just like my father did at about the same age. It is interesting that both of us never snored below that age. In my father's case, the snoring would be compounded with drunkenness and would be so loud that one could hear him from as far as fifty meters or more. I am sure my mother endured several sleepless nights and must have tried in vain to wake him up as Rose would do many years later. In my case, I would often hear my own snoring and would wake up to adjust my pillow as it had become evident to me that the snoring happened whenever my neck was somehow twisted. However, there were many instances when Rose would also be disturbed by my snoring that she couldn't sleep unless she woke me up to adjust. This snoring must have been a constant source of irritation for Rose but she endured with humility.

*   *   *

I write these things to show that Rose was human, with her own share of weaknesses like all of us although the nature and extent vary from one person to the other. The sad thing about our human nature is that even when we are in the wrong, we always take ourselves to be in the right, for that is what our mind would have dictated; we cannot allow our pride to be punctured. That is the tragedy for which our Lord Jesus Christ died on the cross of Calvary, so that the imperfect may become perfect and the unjust become just…only through his grace

Is it really possible to forgive and forget? If forgiving is a virtue then forgiving and forgetting should be a blessing. Whilst it is acknowledged that human memory always brings up some old events, the trivial and the important, the recent and old, we should not make a conscious effort to remember the wrongs done to us. Remembering for the sake of stalking old wounds can only be counter productive and must be avoided. Otherwise the roles are reversed and the perpetrator becomes the victim. However, it is acknowledged that at times our memory banks bring up such issues. In such cases, we need to make conscious efforts to trivialize the issues and seek God's guidance.

It is unwise for any human being to ever think he or she does not make mistakes. Our very nature testifies to that. Those 'who don't make mistakes' cannot learn anything. It is therefore imperative that for any relationship to work, the parties thereof must realize that they make mistakes and therefore should accommodate correction from those around them. Correction or criticism cannot be equated to condemnation. On the other hand, correction must be done with a view to building and not destroying or condemning. It must be based on love.

*   *   *

We are either born with our weaknesses or we acquire these over time. However, the common thread is that they affect third parties negatively in most instances. Likewise, weaknesses may be either passive or active in the way they are projected. Some are spiteful while others are well intended. In evaluating Rose's weaknesses, I note that they were weaknesses in as far as the other parties were unable to appreciate her position and she was equally stubborn to move her position. On her part, these were always well meant. In the final analysis, she could have achieved much more had she been a little more accommodative and open minded in her approach. There are times when one needs to compromise a little in order to win over others so that they can start to gradually appreciate one's perspective.

However, we should always tolerate one another on the premise that the other person either means well or is not well informed. Even those driven by malice should be accommodated. For Jesus died so that all may be served and have life abundantly. He also said that vengeance was his.

Reference passage; Rom 3:21-24

# 14

## Medical History

Rose was generally a very healthy person and was very particular about the things that affected her health like food, exercise and hygiene. Unfortunately, she was not every consistent on her exercise and dieting routines. However, she would also not expose herself to any danger, perceived or real, knowingly. By contrast, I was rather carefree about such issues. Many times she had to caution me on what I said in public, particularly when discussing politics, and also on hygiene issues.

I am not aware of any childhood illnesses or infirmities Rose may have had. The first physical blemish she had was when she gave birth to Taf*adzwa (Fadzi),* our second child, by caesarean section in 1982. Thereafter, she had two other sections for Kevin and Lynda. This was a sacrifice I would appreciate later in life as these sections were calculated risks she had taken and that left her badly scarred although she never referred to such sacrifice as an issue.

However, in between Tatenda and Fadzi, she went through a traumatic experience when she had a miscarriage in 1980. We were staying in Gwanda then where there were no adequate maternity facilities, so she had to go to Bulawayo for such facilities. Furthermore, one of the reasons for going to Bulawayo was that she was not sure if the foetus was still well as its movements appeared to have stopped. As mentioned earlier, I matured rather late in life. Rose stayed with friends during her one week stay in Bulawayo during which period I did not visit her. The news of the miscarriage was like a non event to me and this bothered her a lot but she only mentioned it to me once, and then, only later in life as an expression of dissatisfaction over another matter. Clearly, I could have handled the matter more maturely.

In addition to the scars from multiple caesarean sections, Rose had problems with a slipped disk in her spine later in life. With time the problem got worse to the extent that she occasionally had sleepless nights. She also suffered from osteoporosis which, however, had significantly improved by the time of her departure due to the calcium supplements she had started taking. Rose also developed arthritis which she managed very well through her diet and the taking in of lots of water. She had stopped eating red meat altogether and the arthritis had disappeared. She also had problems with her knees which tended to give way when undue pressure was applied to them, particularly when playing sport.

Like me, Rose was also on treatment for high blood pressure but this was also under control and was never a threat to her life as she always took her medication religiously.

By far the most serious ailment Rose had was the deep vein thrombosis that first manifested itself in July 2005 when Tatenda and his then fiancée, *Munyaradzi* had visited from Canada in preparation for their then upcoming wedding. Two evenings in a row she failed to complete the 15 step staircase to our bedroom and passed out for about a minute on both occasions. We had to dash her to a local hospital on the second occasion where she was admitted in the intensive care unit for ten days. The diagnosis was that a blood clot was just about to lodge itself into one of the heart valves which could have been fatal had it not been attended to in good time. This was a really frightening moment for me as I was scared I would lose her.

Since then she had frequently struggled with the thrombosis problem although she had a very good doctor looking after her. At times the medication would make her blood too thin resulting in internal bleeding while stopping the medication would result in the thickening of the blood, a situation that would risk further clotting. It was a difficult balancing act which was always a source of constant worry for both of us. One wonders if she would have survived long with this condition following the intensive internal bleeding she suffered after the road traffic accident as this would have resulted into a proliferation of blood clots into her blood system.

In hindsight, it would now appear God spared Rose's life so that she could witness Tatenda's and Munyaradzi's wedding a year later, one of the happiest moments of her life. Fifteen months after the wedding, she was taken away from me. I wish to thank God for the extra 28 months between 2005 and 2007 that he allowed me to enjoy her companionship.

Of particular note is that Rose was obsessed with hygiene, per earlier note. A good example was our shower cubicle. I have always taken it to be good practice to use bathroom slippers when showering but had limited this to public facilities. Rose always insisted that we use the slippers even at home. That alone was not enough precaution; we had to turn the sleepers upside down after the shower so that no fungus would grow. Initially, I had problems remembering to turn them over and she would not tire in reminding me that I had not done so. I was generally not impressed as I didn't see the need; I didn't think fungus would grow to risky levels in one day. Eventually it became a reflex and that way I bought my peace.

In addition to washing fruits, hands were to be washed with soap before eating anything. She always discouraged me from buying roast mealies (corn) by the road side as she argued that the vendors had nowhere to wash their hands and that the mealies would have been exposed to pollutants all day. At first I didn't appreciate the significance but I am now her obedient disciple having appreciated the benefits.

It is seemingly the not so careful who are blessed with long life. Life is a gift from God; we cannot claim it by our actions, noble or foolish.

I raise these issues to show that although Rose had these ailments; it was none of these that took her life. She did what was humanly possible to live long but she left us unexpectedly yet many others who have no clue about their health requirements are still around, with some living to ripe old ages. Life is an irony. Somewhat, I am convinced that even if she had not been involved in that fatal accident, somehow, her day had come and no one could have prevented her departure. Who knows, I could have come home to find a corpse in bed.

It is also not age that determines when we pass on otherwise children would not die before those who are in their nineties. We often think that being a good person or a Christian will earn us a long life from God. If it were so, then Lazarus, the friend of Jesus would not have died so young. I take it that for Lazarus to be a special friend of Jesus, he must have been a God fearing person like his sisters, Mary and Martha. Although Jesus also socialized with sinners, in many cases he did so with the objective of converting them to his ways. Of course, Lazarus was eventually brought back to life by Jesus, as a way of demonstrating the power of God.

On the other hand, when one dies early in life it does not necessarily mean that one has not been blessed. Instead, it could actually be a blessing to die young as only God knows why one has to die at that particular moment in time. We need to simply know and accept that life is a gift from God which he can withdraw at any time without justifying himself to anyone.

Dying may actually be a reward for the soul.

Reference passages; Matt 8:9, Luke 17: 7-9, Eph 6:5-9, Col 3:22-25

# 15

## Blessings from the Lord

Marriage between a man and a woman was instituted by God in the Garden of Eden (Genesis 2:24) and witnessed and endorsed by Jesus when he attended the wedding at Cana where he performed his first miracle by turning water into high quality wine (John 2:1-11). While history is replete with married couples who failed to have children, secular and Christian alike, the majority of mankind have been blessed with the gift of children. **Children are therefore not the reason for, but the result of marriage and only as blessings from God (Genesis 1:28).** Put differently, we do not marry in order to have children but we have children because we are married and those marriages have been blessed by God in a special way. However, the omniscient God loves children born out of wedlock as much as he loves any other, including those born out of rape cases. If it were not so, Jesus would have excluded such children in his numerous references to the humility of little children. See Mat. 18:4, Mat 19: 14 and Mark 10:16.

Stories have been told of married couples or individuals who have spent fame and fortune in order to have a child as well as those who have been so callous as to kill their only child, not appreciating that having a child is probably the best blessing one can ever have. Modern technology has helped those who, under normal circumstances, would not have had any hope of having a child to have one. I urge the childless couples not to despair, for their very unions are blessings from God which must be cherished. Like any blessing, children are not availed to all who want them. Let glory be given to God in all circumstances.

Going by Genesis 1:28 and Ecclesiastes 12:13, I am inclined to believe that God blessed man with children and the love to care for those children so that his favoured species may continue to multiply for the sake of worshipping him. He, therefore, gave all other living creatures the ability to multiply, as well as the love for their offspring, for the sake of man to whom he gave dominion over them. I am sure many have seen, either in real life or on television documentaries, the extent to which animals would go to defend their young ones from predators. Without such love, very few of the offspring would survive, thus threatening the survival of their species.

It is in this context that Rose and I considered ourselves blessed when the Lord gave us four beautiful children. Rose was extremely proud of them as much as I am. Unfortunately, she did not spend as much time with them as she would have wanted due to her industrious disposition. Also, as a nurse, there were times when she would come home late and tired or work night duty leaving her with very little time to bond with the children. The children therefore bonded with me a lot faster and related with me with ease.

While they have already been introduced in earlier chapters it is appropriate that I show how Rose related to them individually and how they have generally turned out to be.

## Tatenda Bryan

Born 30 June 1978, Tee (as we call him) was the one who 'broke his mother's virginity', as my mother would say of me, being the first born child. He therefore occupied a special place in his mother's life which no other child could claim. As was to be expected, not only Rose and I were excited by his arrival, but the whole clan, for he was destined to carry the family name. While he was an average child, we found it peculiar that he started to walk when he was barely nine moths old. He always wanted his independence as he would play alone without bothering anyone. He would demonstrate this quest for independence by refusing to be lifted or to be carried once he learnt how to walk. We would be going somewhere on foot and he would be delaying us due to his slower pace. I would then lift him up whereupon he would protest by screaming and kicking until I put him down. He would then walk back to the spot where I would have picked him up, or deliberately go beyond the spot for good measure, and then start walking towards us at an even slower pace. We have all had good fun over it over the years. This trait manifested itself very early when he weaned himself off from mother's milk and from both our laps as soon as he started to walk, in search of adventure, I suppose. While I tried to hold on to him, Rose was happy to see him leave home in search of further independence.

Tee is *Mr. Smart*. Although he is generally smart intellectually and physically, he has not done justice to his educational career. After obtaining 8 A's at 'Ordinary Level' he is yet to embark on a tertiary qualification, preferring to work without any. Understandably, this was a source of disappointment for his mother and I have also expressed my displeasure at this state of affairs. He tends to procrastinate, like me.

His wedding to Munyaradzi in 2007 was one of Rose's most exciting moments in life. Where we had previously had two daughters, we now had three. The couple was blessed with little

Ethan Tatenda on January 20, 2009. I pray that they do realize that he is a gift and blessing from God which should not be taken for granted but cherished at all times. It is really cruel irony that with the way Rose loved children; she is not around to see our first grandchild. Tatenda and Munyaradzi are currently staying in Toronto, Canada.

## Tafadzwa Thelma

Fadzi was born on 1 April 1982 by caesarean section, the gap between her and Tatenda largely being due the miscarriage that Rose had in 1980. After a four year wait, her arrival was special. She was also special in that she was the first girl child.

Fadzi is the emotional type who, in contrast to Tee, took time to get off my lap. She would dash over to me as soon as I returned home from the office and it would always be a struggle to take her off. She liked to be cuddled and in turn would pat and kiss me often. She was so adorable.

As she was growing up it was clear that she was as industrious as her mother and brought a lot of joy to Rose. While she was average in class, Fadzi compensated that with hard work and it has paid off as she has now completed her first university degree with majors in Finance and International Business. She is currently based in Melbourne, Australia where she is working for an insurance company. She has matured very fast and has a striking resemblance of her mother in her determination to achieve goals.

Although Fadzi is *Miss Candid* and calls a spade a spade, she balances this well with being kind hearted. She is focused and makes firm decisions. Beneath that veneer of softness is a tenacity that, when provoked, will leave many surprised. She exudes warmth, is affectionate and expects reciprocity from those around her.

Although away from home, she has assumed the role of mother of the house as she often marshals her siblings whenever there is something to be done at home.

## Kevin Tawanda

When Rose was heavy with Kevin, she had a very strong craving for clay. I would often accompany her to the virgin land adjacent to Msasa Park suburb in Kwekwe, looking for freshly made white-ant mounds. We would then carry loads of it which she would dry in the stove warmer, ground to powder and store in jars in the pantry. She would take this powder for her dessert most evenings only stopping a month or so after Kevin's birth. I understand that the craving meant that the child had a high affinity for minerals which are found in this clay which are required for the formation of strong bones. Rose therefore had a special place for Kevin in her heart.

Kevin was born in Kwekwe on 18 March 1984, also by caesarean section. I recall that he weighed nearly 4kg at birth and that the nurses at the local clinic had to stop recording his weight on the child health card as his weight had gone well out of range.

As a newly born baby, he would literally give us sleepless nights as he would cry ceaselessly. After about a month, to our relief, my mother advised us that he was not getting adequate food from his mother's milk, hence the continuous crying. After initially expressing her doubts, Rose immediately started him on milk formulas and porridge and that bought us our peace! The change was dramatic. As a toddler, he would continue eating any form of soil he would come across as the craving for minerals took time to wane. That unfortunately soured the relationship with his mother who, naturally, detested dirt. Kevin has grown up into a big man..

Like Fadzi, he was very fond of me to the extent that even on the occasions that I would smack him for some misdemeanour, he would immediately dash back to my lap as if nothing had happened, chatting as usual. Whenever he wanted to tell me something, which was often, he would go; "Daddy, daddy, daddy, daddy, daddy, daddy...!" without giving me a chance to respond. It was simply impossible to ignore him.

Rose objected strongly to Kevin's mode of dressing when he became a youth although I did not see anything wrong with it. This brought a lot of tension between them. My efforts to reason with Rose were not successful.

Kevin is *Mr. Daring or Comrade* as I occasionally call him. He is hardly scared of anyone and will do whatever he wants. While he is focused on his goals, he also procrastinates. Although I would not say he is selfish, he needs to consider other people's points of view and feelings for a balanced outlook to life. Kevin also needs to appreciate advice and counselling from family members. Although music is his passion and he has been doing very well with his music degree which he was taking from a university in Melbourne, Australia, he is yet to complete it. I am worried that he may be ruined by some of the vices attendant in the entertainment world.

Kevin is extremely sociable and so daring that he can make friends with anyone, literally, in no time at all. He never runs out of ideas for discussion.

## Lynda Tariro (Lily)

Born on 2 October 1986 by caesarean section, my last born, Lynda, is *Miss Innocent*. She is so sweet 'everyone' hates to hurt her. She wouldn't hurt a fly as the saying goes. Like her mother before her, she expects the world to be perfect. She needs to look at the world differently before she is hurt, for the world out there can be cruel.

As the last child, Rose had a special place for Lily, although she was the most independent of the lot as a baby. She was the exact opposite of Kevin and Fadzi and more like Tee as she would always play alone. Rose and I would, on separate occasions, take her up to our laps and play with her but she would slip away in no time. She would hardly cry unless something was really wrong with her. She has maintained that trait into adulthood although she is now not very different from her siblings. She only learnt to hug us when she had started high school; otherwise she had always deprived us of that affection, no matter how much we tried.

One incident that amused me as she grew up was when Rose and I went fishing with her and a cousin of mine, Lawrence Gabilo. On our way back Lynda started crying from the back seat of the car and we wondered why that was so, only to discover that she was being chocked by the smell of beer that Lawrence was taking. Lynda had never smelt nor come close to alcohol until that day when she was already in junior high school. My remark was; "I hope and pray that you will not be married to a drunkard, my daughter, for life can be cruel." This remains my prayer for all my children.

Lynda is also focused and cannot be moved from her desires once her mind is set. She has always been clear on what she wants in life. She is currently in a second year of an Advertising and Communications degree from a university in Melbourne, Australia.

Lynda has striking emotional and physical resemblance of her mother.

$$* \quad * \quad *$$

Although all my children like quality like their mother, they balance that well with frugality. Another major common characteristic among them is that they are not greedy or selfish, always going out of their way to share whatever they may have, no matter how little. Rose and I used to marvel at how they all used to prefer that the other person be served first or get the only piece of food even when they were all hungry. They neither felt jealousy nor sulked when one of them got the only item or a bigger share ahead of the others. This characteristic manifested itself in very early childhood and has remained in them to this day.

These are the children that God bequeathed to me though Rose. By describing them thus, I am not saying that any one of them is better or worse than the other, or that they are perfect; I am simply looking at the dominant characteristic of each one of them and this is in no way holistic. That they have differences while similar in other respects is a clear testimony of God's wonderfulness. However, they need to know that these characteristics depict both strengths and weaknesses and that it is incumbent upon them to build on the strengths while working on either reducing or eliminating the weaknesses. I pray to God that he may bless their adult life just as he had blessed their mother's and mine. May he bless all their undertakings and may he use them in his plans for the perpetuation of that wonderful species which we call the humans, otherwise known as Homo sapiens.

Reference passages; Gen 17:16, Gen 28:3, Gen 33:5, Job 1:21, Psalm 127:3, Prov 17:6

\*     \*     \*

As I conclude Section One of this book, let me mention that Rose and I rarely prayed as a family, preferring to approach God individually as and when appropriate. By default, our children also adopted this approach. There were many things that we were grateful for as a family and for which we should have thanked God together. Family prayers also help in bonding the family as such prayers help in bringing them as one unit before God. While I always prayed for Rose and the children, it was always in general, without specifically mentioning any of them by name, preferring to simply bundle them together as "my family". I have since learnt to pray specifically for each child and their needs. Maybe God would have heard me if I had prayed directly and specifically for Rose during the time she was under pressure as will be noted in Chapter 17. However, I am comforted by that God already knows all our needs before we bring them before him. It is by grace that he grants us these needs and not necessarily because we ask for them.

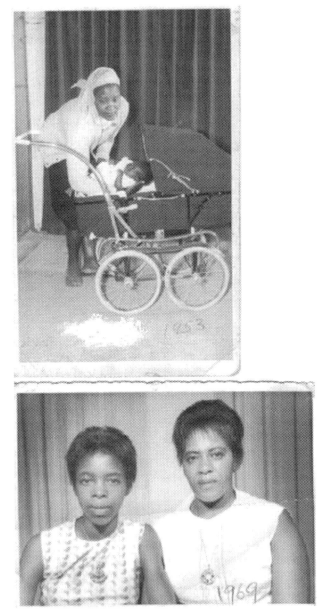

**Top: Rose in cradle roll, 1953**
**Bottom: With Amai , 1969**

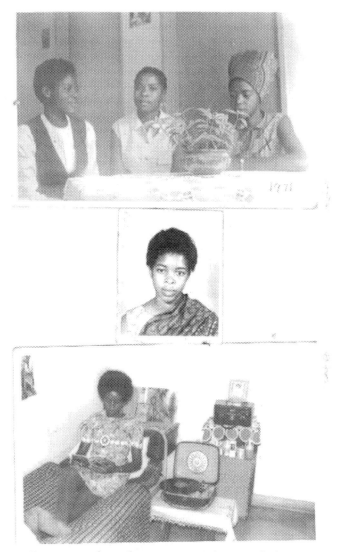

1. Rose at right, admiring pot plant with friends
2. In African attire
3. Studying in her room

1. Matron Eaton at Likuni Hospital (Malawi)
2. With matrons and sisters after graduating at Likuni

**Clockwise from top left**
1. Watching soccer at Babourfields, Bulawayo
2. Dating days with Bryan, 1977
3. Wedding day
4. Wedding day

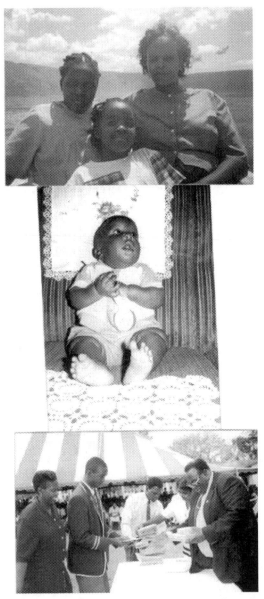

1. With the girls inside Ngorongoro National Park, Tanzania
2. Kevin at 6 months
3. At Tatenda's Prize giving day, Howard Institute

1. Top three; flower arranging for church
2. Pot plants at home

1. Curtains for dining and lounge rooms
2. Cake icing
3. Taking a nap after hard day's work, see pot plant in corner

Clockwise from top left
1. Cooking on open fire at Chiromonye village, Zvishavane
2. Posing for picture at PSMAS
3. With workmates at PSMAS
4. With Bryan at a church seminar

**Back row l to r : Kevin, Tatenda, Tafadzwa and Lynda**
**Front row: Rose and Bryan**

**With Mrs. Maraura, Tatenda's mother-in-law.**

**Rose addressing guests at Tatenda/Munya's wedding**

**Rose with Bryan and newly weds 2007**

The Rose in full bloom ( a year before her departure)

# SECTION TWO

## IN THE SPIRIT

# 16

## Premonitions and Indicators

*As spiritual beings we always receive communication from the world of the spirits. The challenge is that we can never fully comprehend such communication until we, in turn, become spirits.*

I do not claim to have any special powers from any particular source but it is an undeniable fact that some members of my family and I experience dreams pointing to a death whenever one is lurking in the family. I have no idea whatsoever as to the source and purpose of such dreams but they are real and they never lie. Of particular note is that they mainly relate to death although on the odd occasion I also dream whenever I am due to receive an unexpected significant amount of money. Suffice it to say that I have not had the latter type of dream for a long time.

My father, *Mhembedzo* Peter, died of a combination of cerebral malaria and complications arising from hyperacidity in 1978 whilst I was in the process of finalizing my marriage to Rose. Regrettably, he died before seeing his first grandchild, Tatenda, as would happen to Rose thirty years later (her first grandchild came a year after her departure). I was almost becoming a drunkard like him and would not recall if I had any premonitions by way of dreams ahead of his death. If I had any, I was bit irresponsible to appreciate them.

By the time of the death of my maternal grandmother, *Emma Gurai Chingarande (VaGutu)*, in 1998, that of my mother, Eta *Biravira* Matutu *(VaMaSibanda)*, in 2002, that of my paternal grandmother, *Mavhuna* Matutu (*VaGapiro*) in 2005 as well as that of my sister in October of 2007, a pattern had developed where I always knew ahead of time that someone would die in the family. However, I never had the benefit of knowing the identity of the individual concerned. Both my grandfathers died in their ripe old ages when I was still too young to relate to their deaths; *Dovorogwa Chingarande* in 1956 and *Mashavidze Chiromonye* Matutu in 1963.

There are mainly three types of dreams that always portend death for me; a freshly ploughed field without vegetation, a freshly dug up and unfilled grave and a gathering of sombre looking and quiet people, mainly relatives. A fourth one, which I had only heard of but never experienced, the twitching of the upper eyelid of the left eye, started about six weeks ahead of Rose's departure.

Ahead of my mother's death in August 2002, I had continuously dreamt of her crop fields in Zvishavane, newly ploughed and generously applied with rich organic manure. I must have had this dream, in exactly the same form, no less than ten times in the six months preceding her death, only to stop the day she died! Whilst I had heard of this type of premonition in childhood, I had completely forgotten about it only for it to hit me so hard then. Since then, it has become a pattern; an unwelcome harbinger of terrible news. *VaGapiro's* death was also preceded by dreams of her own ploughed fields, also generously applied with organic manure. I remember telling Rose that I was expecting bad news from Zvishavane any time. Although in many instances the person to whom the dreams relate to remain a mystery, this time around, I knew that it was my grandmother who would be leaving. The news was not long in coming and I was not surprised at all as I was expecting it and was emotionally prepared.

Beginning August 2007, a new wave of similar dreams started. I went into panic mode and shared the dreams with Rose who always comforted me and suggested that they could be just meaningless dreams. I obviously knew otherwise and remained concerned although without a solution. I had an *amainini*, Marceline *Chingarande*, who was critically ill then but who passed on after Rose, early in 2008, who I thought the dreams were pointing at. Whilst it would have been sad to lose her, it would have come as no shock. To some extent I was 'prepared' for any news on her, unwelcome as it would have been. It is now clear that my premonitions appear not to relate to terminally ill individuals, but to those who die unexpectedly.

Then, in early October my sister, Mrs. Berita *Chigavakava* fell seriously ill. I concluded that my dreams could have been pointing to her. Whilst this could have been so, the worst was yet to come. Berita was to die the same month of October after Rose and I had brought her to Harare for treatment. I obviously grieved and cried over her departure, lamenting on how her husband was possibly the source of the disease that took her as he had generally led a reckless life and abused my sister in a manner I cannot describe here. However, I can recount how he abused the Matutu family. They never got formally married as he flatly refused to pay *lobola* as is the norm in our culture. Over the years, they were blessed with three children. On one occasion, when Smarks followed up on the *lobola*, Chigavakava's response was that the seller always has recourse to reclaiming his property in the event the buyer defaults. But with time I had learnt to forgive him as much as she had done. By the time of Berita's departure, she had accepted her fate as she knew she was not responsible for the disease and therefore had no cause for regrets. She also appeared to have forgiven her husband for any wrongs he may have done to her. I was then convinced the dreams had been pointing at her.

During my sister's funeral wake in Kwekwe, my brother, Smarks, confided in me that he had had some dreams that he had been hesitant to share with me for a while. He had persistently dreamt that Rose would depart soon in a violent manner. This was to be the first direct indication of who my dreams were ultimately pointing at. I was obviously worried by this news but was powerless. On the other hand, I wished the dreams away and never considered it as a possible reality that Rose would leave me at all. I even overlooked telling her about it. To this day I don't know if I should have done so. Not that it would have made any difference as we all know that we have no control over our fate although one can always pray to God for deliverance. Maybe if I had shown some form of concern, she could have probed me on the source of such anxiety and the matter could have been discussed in detail. She could have also related this news to the dreams she appeared to have had in the weeks leading to her departure and together with mine, could have been a pointer of some sort. Somehow, we may have been prepared.

To my horror and confusion, my dreams persisted and even intensified after the death of my sister. I discussed this with Rose but she suggested that they could be just that; dreams. Regrettably, I couldn't link Smarks' dreams with mine. However, I remained concerned but helpless. I was a victim of my own dreams and trapped in a cul-de-sac with no way out, incapacitated.

The week leading to Rose's departure was the most intensive and dramatic in terms of these dreams. Firstly, my daughter Fadzi, dreamt that I had visited her at her place of work and on enquiring why I was there I had told her that I had come to advise that her mother had had a fatal road traffic accident. Whatever power it is, it transcended the nearly eleven thousand kilometres between Harare and Melbourne to deliver this message to my daughter, ahead of the event! How precise and incredible, even revealing the mode of accident.

My sister, Mrs. *Vongai* Nondo, who stays in Gokwe, which is more than three hundred and fifty kilometres from Harare, whilst sitting in her yard the day before the accident, in what appeared to be a vision, saw a freshly dug but empty grave which immediately disappeared. She could have gone into some sort of a trance to see this vision. Immediately, she anticipated bad news. When she received the news two days later, she was devastated but not surprised.

The unwelcome dreams continued unabated. By far the most dramatic was when on the Tuesday of the fateful week, my two late grandmothers and my mother whom I have mentioned earlier, came to me in a dream, in single file. The trio drifted from the left in a descending direction and stopped immediately in front of me with *VaGutu* in front followed by *VaGapiro* and lastly *VaMaSibanda*. They appeared in their portrait form as if something was blocking the lower part of their bodies. They all looked at me with gloomy faces without saying a word and immediately drifted away to my right before disappearing back into the sky. It was as if they came from and left for Heaven. When I awoke I was very confused and worried as to the content and significance of their message but never had a chance to discuss it with Rose as she was extremely busy with her studies. Maybe it was never meant that Rose and I should discuss these issues in the first place. In retrospect, it would appear they had come to warn me that someone from my family would join them into the world of the spirits. Alternatively, they could have come to announce that they were ready to receive someone into their world. Further still, going by their gloomy faces, they could have come to commiserate with me. I am a Christian who has never worshipped ancestral spirits my whole life. I simply do not believe in them as that is idol worshiping. However, somehow, the spirits from the dead appear to follow my life without being solicited. This is a phenomenon which I do not have any control over. Although *VaGapiro* was never a Christian, she was an extremely kind and humble person. The other two were devout Christians and it therefore puzzles me to this day how their spirits would team up to visit me in this manner.

Where exactly did they come from and how was I to know their message when they never spoke to me? Did God send them? I am convinced that Rose is in heaven right now, so where do my three forbearers come in? What was I supposed to do about it? Is it a gift or a curse that I have such premonitions?

The same week I dreamt of a freshly dug and empty grave just like my sister would do later in the week. Once again, I was dumbfounded but told no one and did not act on it.

I have a nephew, Melody Mnikwa, who stays in Masvingo, over two hundred kilometres south of Harare. His wife dreamt that same week that my brother, Smarks, had brought to her the news of Rose's departure following a road traffic accident. As it turned out, this is exactly how she met her end on this earth, although, instead of a visit from Smarks, they received a phone call.

Then the twitching eyelid started. As mentioned earlier, I had heard of this indicator in childhood but had never experienced it. For almost two months my left eye was twitching regularly. The twitching became more violent and frequent, several times per day, as we approached the fateful day. I discussed the matter with Rose but once again she brushed it aside and I also stopped paying attention to it while deep down it continued to bother me. **Indeed, the twitching eventually stopped, but only after Rose's departure!**

\*     \*     \*

In November 2007, Rose and I visited South Africa for some business and shopping. On our first night, whilst seated in our hotel room in Polokwane and quite awake, I saw the two of us in what appeared like a recurrent dream, driving on a highway and taking a detour that came to a dead end. When it persisted, I told Rose about it. The following day, all our efforts at transacting our business wherever we went were unsuccessful. The second night, I dreamt of my late grandfather, *Mashavidze Chiromonye* (what a fine gentleman he was), using a very long hide whip to hit the roof of a thatched hut others and I were in. When I asked him what he was doing, he said that he was blessing the occupants of the hut (his first name means one who blesses and provides for others). The following day, everything we had failed to accomplish the previous day went like clockwork. We drove to Pretoria without any directions (this was our first time to go beyond Polokwane), and headed straight to the place where we accomplished our business transactions without any hitches and drove back to Polokwane the same day. The following day, we concluded our business in Polokwane and returned home.

\*     \*     \*

Among the items recovered from Rose's office was a book titled "Understanding the Dreams you Dream". This was the first time for me to see this book as it was brand new, suggesting it had just been bought. I doubt however that she found the book to be of much use. This however suggested that she may have had some unusual dreams in the days ahead of her departure which she was seeking to understand. One of her friends confirmed that she indeed was always talking of dreams for which she was searching meanings. She had also shared meanings of some other dreams in general. Another friend of hers mentioned that Rose had recently confided in her that she had just become scared of driving, particularly holding the steering wheel. As fate would have it, it was the car that took her life and specifically the steering wheel that crushed her chest.

Regrettably, her studies continued to be a barrier between us as neither of us was able to discuss these strange happenings. I suppose the busy schedule was part of the gradual separation process.

\*     \*     \*

My good sister in Christ, *Thulani* Sibanda, would later testify that Rose had mentioned seeing a bright light whenever praying in her last days. She had mentioned that she felt an unusual excitement whenever she saw that light (please refer to the hymn towards the end of this chapter). Somehow, this experience had given Rose a new meaning in life the form of which was still not clear to her. She was therefore ecstatic about her fate, even though by default, not knowing what specifically was in store for her. Although she also mentioned this to me once, unfortunately, we couldn't get to discuss this in detail due the heavy schedule already mentioned.

\*     \*     \*

Rose had quite a sizable collection of clothes, many of them old and no longer in use, all simple and unsophisticated. She also had lots of knitting as well as clothing materials collected over the years. Whenever I looked at this collection I got a chilling and foreboding feeling within me wondering how I would be able to distribute all of it should Rose somehow die before me. (In Zimbabwean culture, all the belongings of a deceased person are distributed to the living the day after the burial although some people prefer to do so on the first anniversary of the death). I have no idea as to what prompted such thoughts as this was well before the dreams started.

*    *    *

As mentioned earlier, I was one of four Elders at Avondale Church of Christ. (I thank God for giving me such an honourable responsibility). On more than one occasion, whilst at church service, I have wondered who among the four elders and/or our spouses would go first... whom among the elders would God decide to take home first and how long this team of elders would remain intact. I have no idea what prompted such thoughts but I considered them to be just wild thoughts without any significance. Were these just mere thoughts or was something or somebody preparing me for what was to be the inevitable. The answer was not long in coming although I was certainly not prepared for it.

*    *    *

Rose had always been a restless sleeper who would always wake up to hunt mosquitoes with her towel (she badly reacted to insecticides) whereas I have always been a sound sleeper. Lately, the roles were somewhat reversed as she became such a heavy sleeper that once asleep, she would only wake up in the morning and she became a bit concerned about it. This was also probably due to exhaustion. She even mentioned that she had problems remembering dreams.

At one time she doubted if she was having any dreams at all. It would appear the dreams for which she was now seeking interpretation were very recent. My concern was that something had drastically changed in her and wondered what it was. It now appears both the heavy schedule and the heavy sleeping were both meant to prepare her for her final sleep.

\*     \*     \*

One day in October 2007, I mentioned to Rose what appeared to have been an obvious statement: that life was strange in that we all go through the various phases of life, from childhood, teenager, young but single adult, married adult, married with children, old age and then suddenly one partner goes, leaving the other behind, alone. 'When one looks back, all this happens over such a short time, as if in a flash, that the purpose of life appears to be obscure,' I reasoned. 'Was this all there was to life?' I wondered if, besides God's primary purpose for us of worshipping him ceaselessly, if he didn't create us simply to perpetuate the human species by giving us offspring and the accompanying love that will make us care for such offspring without a murmur, whatever the circumstances, in pursuant of his objective( of being worshiped). Once the latter is achieved, one partner departs while the other lingers on until his or her time comes. Meanwhile, the cycle is replicated many times over, even during our life time through subsequent generations, all for the sake of worshipping God. Once again, I have no idea what prompted me to think and say that but what sounded like casual talk turned out to be prophetic. She has done her part in worshipping God and helped in the perpetuation of human species so that God may continue to be worshipped. That's all there is for mankind. Meanwhile, I am left behind, alone.

\*     \*     \*

Rose always insisted on personally washing my undergarments and socks as she rightly felt it was improper for the house maid to do so. I would have done it if she had allowed me to but I did not insist. Obviously I was being spoiled. Once in a while I would wash these whenever she appeared busy. About a month before her departure, as if by design and in preparation for her departure, and may be because she was too busy, I started doing this chore in earnest. Occasionally I washed her garments as well. once again, I was being

*   *   *

It has been said that procrastination is the thief of time. I am guilty as charged on this one. Rose had always wanted us to have a gazebo in our front yard. As I mentioned earlier, I procrastinated until one day three years ago when she remonstrated with me for not caring about her wishes. I quickly arranged for the construction of the gazebo and a really beautiful structure ensued with which both of us were extremely pleased. One feature of the gazebo is the wood fired brick stove, with oven and fire place facilities. These facilities were to prove very invaluable during her funeral wake as it was raining heavily and there was no electricity for most of that period. Had she not insisted that the gazebo be constructed, food preparation would have been adversely affected a great deal. By default, she was planning for the gathering. Our house is also relatively big so much that no one spent the nights in the open as is the practice at many such events. God's providence is simply wonderful.

Related to the gazebo was the provision of firewood. We have a vegetable greenhouse in our back yard and over the years we had wanted to have the tall blue gum trees just behind the greenhouse removed as they appeared to interfere with the growth of vegetables. A year ago I managed to convince the management of the club on whose property the trees grew to have them removed and this was duly done. We acquired  most of the timber for firewood; I even remarked then that we had enough firewood to last many years even if we had a huge gathering at home. The gathering was not long in coming and the firewood became God sent. It would appear my words had once again been prophetic.

*   *   *

A few yeas ago, the Elders at Avondale Church of Christ decided that we study the Bible from Genesis to Revelations in our cell groups. In our cell group, we set ourselves some milestones for the Old Testament and these included the return of Israel from Egyptians bondage as well as the return from Babylonian captivity and of course, the prophets. It was my brother in Christ, Eubert Mashaire, who used to joke that he would not be around 'to witness the return of the children of Israel from Egyptian bondage'. We all used to have fun about it saying that he would be surprised that those least expected might be gone ahead of him. Whilst we joked about it, there was always that chilling probability that this could actually happen and eventually, it had to be my Rose. She had her preferred chair whenever we visited the Mashaire home for Bible study in which she would doze on most of the occasions. Lately, I have decided to sit in that chair in her memory whenever I visit. As mentioned earlier, the dozing was due to her heavy and punishing work schedule, both at the office and at home. Of course, I cannot erase the memories but at least I can minimize visualizing her in that chair as I will be occupying it.

*   *   *

Of our four children, only Lynda, the last born, did not go to boarding school for her secondary education with Rose preferring to have her at home for company. Lynda did not like this arrangement as she thought that she was missing out on 'benefits' that go with being a boarder like 'more' pocket money and just being away from household chores. What she didn't realize was that she got more pocket money because she could always get instant help whenever she ran out. When Lynda completed high school, circumstances were such that she had to spend another year with us before joining others abroad for university. Rose never missed an opportunity to express how happy she was that things had turned out that way. Clearly, it was not accidental that this happened but God's plan for the two to bond well before Rose's departure. With time and in retrospect, Lynda now appreciates that she had that opportunity to bond with her mother (please refer the Lynda's letter in Chapter 23).

\*　　\*　　\*

Five days before Rose's departure, my brother Lazarus arrived from Australia with his wife Sandra and two daughters, *Kuzivakwashe* and *Tanaka* after an absence of seven years from Zimbabwe. It was meant to be a great Christmas reunion. In retrospect, it would appear they had come for a great farewell. Later, I was to wonder as to the power that had prompted them to come at that specific time after so many years of absence. Had they come to bid farewell to Rose, I still wonder. I will touch more on this later.

\*　　\*　　\*

It would appear that God had to wait for Tatenda's and Munyaradzi's wedding in August 2006, before taking her, for that was one of Rose's happiest moment. She was later to share her happiness with me and many of her friends for quite some time. No doubt, she had her views of the newly weds' future and probably visualized playing with her grandchildren not in the too distant future. This was not to be. Fifteen months later, she was no more. Whilst seeing one out of four possible weddings would be too low by our standards, it is probably very high by God's view.

One day after the wedding, I called Tatenda aside to advise him that now that he was married, he must realize that he will inherit the headship of the family in the not too distant future.

"One never knows, anything could happen to your mother or me", I told him.

He remonstrated with me suggesting that such things should never be mentioned and that it made him nervous. Just over a year later, this was to be a reality. Had this been another prophecy?

*       *       *

The local government authority has two cemeteries, Warrens Hills, which is relatively more secure and central and Granville which is not so secure and is on the outskirts of Harare. They have discontinued the practice of allowing people to have a number graves reserved for their families as the demand for such facility is now far outstripping supply. Over the past few years Rose and I had been to Warren Hills a number of times to bury a number of friends and relatives. On each occasion I would notice that the preferred side was filling up fast and I would wonder where Rose and I would be buried when our time came. Sadly, the irony was that it now appeared to be a matter of first come first served as the cemetery was fast filling up, as if dying had suddenly become an honour, I thought to myself.

'Did one have to die now in order to be buried in the preferred section as the ever increasing number of new graves seemed to suggest', I wondered. I knew that this was a wild, trivial, irrelevant as well as reckless thought but at times we cannot steer our thoughts from their course. So indeed it became first come first served for my Rose. In no time, she was to secure her place at Warren Hills. But the first come first served status she got was from heaven where I am sure she has been accommodated ahead of us all who remain behind.

*   *   *

Over the thirty years of our marriage, Rose rarely appreciated clothing bought for her in her absence as she was rather too selective on what she wanted. Consequently, I rarely went shopping with her because I knew I would be frustrated by going from shop to shop looking for was clearly not available. In 2005 I visited Australia in order to attend the graduation ceremony of our daughter Tafadzwa. With the assistance of Lazarus' wife, Sandra, I bought Rose a very expensive costume which I thought she would like. She certainly liked the dress but it needed some minor alterations. Although I reminded her several times that she needed to wear that costume, she kept putting the matter off until at one time I challenged her to tell me if she did not like it considering the few hundred dollars spent on it. Her response was that the dress was too nice anyway that even if she altered it, she would not have an occasion to put it on. Ultimately, she had occasion to put it on; at the funeral parlour! It would now appear as if the dress had been bought specifically for that occasion. Not that it made any significant difference whether or not she had put on an old dress. I am sure that in her humility, she would have preferred an older dress but I felt that it would be appropriate for her to put it on, on her final journey.

*   *   *

In August 2007 I lost a significant amount of money to a conman which I am still struggling to recover. He had been introduced to me by a very trusted friend and I had no reason to suspect that the transaction would go wrong. The last time I met him (his first name is *Bongani* with a surname starting with Mb) my parting words to him were to the effect that he was a harbinger of bad news and that I was likely to have deaths in the family because such a deed was inconceivable and had never happened in my family. Besides the huge amount involved, this was the first time I had been conned. Interestingly, his name means 'be grateful'. Just as well, a name is just that, a name. Otherwise I would wonder who between him and me should be grateful from this transaction. I am a general believer in the human race; that on average, humans must trust one another otherwise life will cease to be what it is known to be. Granted, exceptions are always there but they remain just that, exceptions, and are unwelcome. Within a period of four months, I had lost two very close members of the family, my sister and my dear wife. I trust that Bongani has the opportunity to read this book and that it jogs his memory of my parting words. While I wish him well in his life and have always prayed for him, let him also realize that I still expect him to pay my money back so that this chapter may be closed.

*    *    *

One of the more dramatic premonitions which had not been brought to my attention earlier was when Rose requested a church friend, one early morning, to sing with her over the telephone a hymn we used to sing at Dadaya way back in the sixties. The hymn which is captured below, when paraphrased, refers to the light one sees when heaven's gates are opened and how one wishes to go through those gates. It would appear that the gates had been opened for Rose and that God was beckoning her to go through. Regrettably, there is no known English version of this hymn but juxtaposed is a crude translation which I hope will be of help. There are also no written music notes although the author knows how it is sung.

| Pasuwo Rakashamapo | The Open Gate |
|---|---|
| *Pasuwo rakashamapo* | There, on that open gate |
| *Ndowonawo chiedza* | I see a bright light |
| *Chinobva Gorgota uko* | That comes from Golgotha |
| *She wakachitungidza* | Set alight by the Saviour |
| | |
| *Chorus* | Chorus |
| *Inyasha huru iyeyo* | For by God's mighty grace |
| *Ndingandopinda ipapo* | I may enter therein |
| *Neni! neni!* | Even me, even me |
| *Ndingandopindawo* | Yes, I may enter therein |
| | |
| *Rakashamira ipapo* | It is wide open |
| *Vodo kuuya vose* | They all want to come |
| *Vachena navapfumiwo* | The rich and the poor |
| *Marudzi ose ose* | All nations are welcome |
| | |
| *Musatye henyu, chiuyai* | Do not be afraid, come all |
| *Mugozopinda naro* | Through that open gate |
| *Kudenga She uchamupai* | The Lord will give you |
| *Korona yomufaro* | The crown of joy up yonder |
| | |
| *Bva seri kwaro ikweyo* | Beyond that beautiful gate |
| *Kuchema kunosiiwa* | Crying will be forgotten |
| *Tichandoona Jesu' ko* | We shall see Jesus up there |
| *Uko kunofariwa* | The place of endless joy |

It is clear that it was not by accident that she sang this hymn at the time that she did, and that she was already in another sphere of life. She was looking forward to joining her Lord, albeit without her being conscious of it. She was ready and fully dressed up for her final journey. Like Apostle John, her spiritual eyes had been opened so that she could see that which has been reserved for the chosen few. Of that, I have no doubt.

When all has been said and done, strange and unnatural revelations took place and we were denied the opportunity to evaluate them, not that we had the capacity and wherewithal to do so. The general thread was that they were all advance warnings of the imminent departure of my dear wife. However, no amount of expended human effort would have changed things that had already been fixed by God. However, when I consider the answered prayer as captured in Chapter 19 and the events surrounding King Hezekiah, I am inclined to think that God would have spared Rose's life if I had prayed for her earnestly ( see 2 Kings 20:1-11 and Isaiah 38).

I have no idea of what prompts premonitions and why some people experience them while others do not, even in the same family. All I know is that, while coming in various forms, they are real, at least to me. The common thread as far as mine are concerned is that they mainly relate to individuals who would be generally fit and strong and not to the terminally ill. Thus, the premonitions I had, starting August 2007, do not appear to have related to my sister and my aunt who were both terminally ill, but to Rose. Similarly, when my mother and my grandmother passed on, I had similar premonitions because both were generally fit when these started. It is clear therefore that such premonitions are meant to be warnings about the unexpected deaths and not about those already considered imminent.

Reference passages; Job 14:5, Rom 1:10, 1 Cor 4:19, 1 Cor 16:7, James 4:15

# 17

## Events leading to the fateful day

*As much as I was not aware of the moment of my birth, I may never be aware of my fate. My departure will be as miraculous as my arrival.*

As mentioned earlier, Rose was in her final year of a degree program with a local university and was therefore working on her research paper as well as preparing for her end of semester exams. To say that she was under pressure would be a gigantic understatement but being the conscientious person she was, she took everything in her stride.

She had established a tight daily routine. She would get up as early as 4 a.m. to prepare breakfast before electricity was switched off by the supplying authority around 05:00hrs and to study for the exams before getting off to work. During lunch break she would go into a corner in her office, out of sight of the passer byes, and study. Soon after work she would proceed to join a friend or two for a group study or sharing notes for the project. Dinner time was around 8 p.m. when she would arrive home before catching a nap on the couch as soon as she sat down. I would then wake her up about 22:00hrs when we would proceed to the office where I would type her research papers and discuss with her any corrections that would need to be done. This would see us retiring to bed around midnight although in many cases she would remain behind to polish up and plan for the following day. This was indeed a punishing routine for her for about two and half weeks. Eventually, it took its toll on her. The funeral wake that she had to attend in Highfield as mentioned below compounded a situation that was already bad.

As mentioned earlier, Lazarus and family arrived in the midst of all this. A day after their arrival, our daughter in law's grandmother, *Mbuya* Maraura passed away and for two nights we joined the Maraura's at the funeral wake. It is Zimbabwean practice for friends and relatives to spend whole nights at a wake only going back home in the morning for a bath and breakfast before proceeding to their offices. I have never appreciated this practice even for someone close to me. For two nights I, with some help from her dear friend, Mrs. Maraura, our daughter-in-law's mother, successfully persuaded Rose to go home with me. However, on the 1 December 2007 she insisted on spending the night there and my efforts at persuading her otherwise were rather muted as I knew I had no chance of succeeding and I proceeded home without her with the intention of picking her up first thing the following morning. I was not happy leaving her behind, knowing what she had gone through.

Meanwhile, Lazarus had arranged for Auline, his sister in law who stays in South Africa, to bring us some groceries for Christmas as these were in critical short supply in Zimbabwe. We were grateful for the gesture. The following day, the 2nd of December 2007, was a Sunday when I had plans to go to church. My plans were to pick Rose up and bring her home to sleep whilst I proceeded to church where I was presiding. After service I would then pick Rose up for the burial of *Mbuya* Maraura. As I was on my way to Highfield Suburb to collect Rose I got a message on my phone suggesting that I collect Auline from Roadport, the Harare international bus terminus. I then decided to collect Auline before proceeding to Highfield so that we could drop her off at her sister's in Kuwadzana before proceeding home. The bus, which was supposed to arrive at 6 a.m., did not arrive on time, so I proceeded to Highfield, picked Rose up and returned for Auline. At Highfield, I found Rose waiting for me at the deceased's neighbour's home. Of major interest is the humility that I saw on her face as she greeted me that morning. Although she had always been a humble person, this was different…it was intense. She was even avoiding direct eye contact with me. I also marvelled at the humility with which she bid farewell to the lady of that house. I don't think I will ever forget that experience. In hindsight, I now think that she was carrying out her last act of service to mankind, as if she knew her fate(please refer to letter 3 of Chapter 23).

At one time I sent a message on my cell phone to Never Sibanda, one of the elders at Avondale, suggesting that he presides over the service if I was unduly delayed. (How I now wish I had done just that). The bus had not arrived by 7:45 a.m. when I suggested to Rose that she drops me home so that she could return for Auline (that was the fatal mistake both of us made and regrettably that was the last time I saw Rose in her sound body). Little did I know that she had not had as much as a wink the whole night due to overcrowding and the all night singing vigil.

The bus had still not arrived by the time Rose returned to Roadport, only eventually arriving after 8 a.m. having reportedly been delayed due to a breakdown. Evidently Rose was extremely tired and sleepy when we parted and we both made serious errors of judgment as she should never have undertaken that assignment.

One would now wonder if these events, including her heavy schedule and the delayed bus, were the means or the cause of

Rose's demise. I am inclined to believe that these were the means to what was inevitable. I therefore feel that even if any of these events had not taken place, Rose would have still departed on that day. A story is told of a real life incident when a man dreamt that he had been crashed to death by a motor vehicle. The dream had been so vivid that it left him really scared. He resolved that he was not going to leave his bedroom that day as a way of preventing exposure to vehicular traffic. As events unfolded, a heavy vehicle which was driving past his house veered off the road and rammed straight into his bedroom. He died on the spot. His fate had been decided. Who are we therefore to question when and how we should leave this world?

I am reminded of the words of Job in Job Chapter 14: 5 where he says; "Since his (human being) days are numbered, the number of his months is with you, you have appointed his limits, so that he cannot pass."

Who am I now to suggest that events should have taken a different course in order to save her from her fate? The limit had been set and no one had the authority to vary it.

It also made me to appreciate the prefix used by some people before they embark on something; "God willing, I will do such and such". This is taken from James 4: 13-17. Whatever our plans may be, they can only succeed if God wills so. On our own, they remain just that; plans. According to Genesis Chapter 1 verse 28, God said to Adam, "Be fruitful and multiply; fill the earth and subdue it; have dominion over the fish of the sea, over the birds of the air and over every living thing that moves on earth." Since that day in the Garden of Eden, man has abrogated to himself more power than was granted to him by God. We forget that on our own we are nothing and can do nothing; that our very lives are in God's hand. How many of us have realized that from the day of our birth, each day that follows brings us nearer to our death.

Even as we celebrate our birthdays, year in and year out, we are in fact celebrating our imminent departure from this earth. Yet we tend to dread that day and when it comes, those remaining wail without hope. We also know that only God knows the limit he has set for each one of us. It could be a second, a day, a week, a year or even another fifty years from today. With the limit already set and imminent, we should therefore behave appropriately and should always defer to God by saying, 'God willing, I will be alive tomorrow to do such and such'. That way when death comes our way, it doesn't catch us and those around us by surprise. Except for God's grace we may not be here tomorrow.

Reference passages; James 4:13-17, Luke 12: 13-21

# 18

## My World Falls Apart

*If we were of this world we would not suffer just as the redeemed soul will not suffer when it returns to its abode.*

Rose proceeded to take Auline to Kuwadzana Township and whilst there, she expressed her tiredness. Lazarus and his family had spent the night at Kuwadzana and could therefore not have picked Auline as they had no car to use. She proceeded home, more than ten kilometres away, for her sleep. Meanwhile, I was coordinating the church service. Soon after the business meeting I dashed home supposedly to pick Rose for the burial service. I got home around 11:45 a.m. only to note that her car was not in the garage. Right away, my heart sank, fearing for the worst. The error of my judgment became very evident. I dashed into the house and enquired from the housemaid on Rose's whereabouts. The maid advised that Rose had not returned since morning. My fears were confirmed; something terrible had happened to her, most likely a road traffic accident. I could not phone her as all our cell phones had not been charged as we had had no electricity for six days. I sat, sunk in the chair, not knowing how to proceed or where to go. Within ten minutes, I received a telephone call from a nephew in Karoi, advising that Rose had been involved in a life threatening road traffic accident and had been taken to Parirenyatwa Hospital in Harare.

I quickly dashed to the hospital's casualty department and was taken to the X-Ray room where they had taken her. They quickly returned her to the recovery room where they explained to me that she had suffered severe multiple fractures to her left ankle, the right femur and hip bones. They showed me the x-rays and even my uninitiated eyes could tell that the femur had been badly splintered. She also had a deep cut on her right shin which however, did not bleed much, even before it had been sutured. This left me a bit puzzled. They assured me that both the head and the chest had been cleared of internal injuries. What was now left was to identify the Orthopaedic doctor who was to attend to her fractures and they assured me that today's technology was very good in that area. Somewhat I was reassured although with some reservations. Meanwhile Never Sibanda and his wife, *Thulani*, had arrived as well as Rose's immediate superior at work. We all agreed that although the medical facilities at the hospital were not quire satisfactory, it was too early to move Rose to another hospital as there were still a lot of investigations underway. The other hospitals were unlikely to have their full compliment of doctors as this was a weekend. Moreover, being a teaching hospital, there were more than adequate doctors and nurses attending to her. I even commended them for the commitment to duty as evidenced by the manner they ran around attending to her. This later proved to be wrongly placed gratitude as proven by events which unfolded the following day.

Meanwhile she had been heavily sedated to help her manage the pain. She mentioned to me that she was in a lot of pain, particularly in the chest. The doctors once again reassured me that the chest and head had been cleared of internal injuries. When I told her that she had three fractures in her legs she was surprised as she had no feeling in her legs and had no recollection of the accident. I am not sure that she recognized me then. They started suturing the non-bleeding deep cut in the shin. They then wheeled her to the Orthopaedic ward where they quickly put her on traction and intravenous fluids as well as giving her another dose of pain killing drugs. Lazarus had by then joined me at the hospital as I had earlier on sent him to notify Rose's mother, *Gogo MaNcube*, of the accident. She was not home. When he returned, it was now evening and I received a telephone call advising that Collet's (my brother) children had arrived from Mutare and needed to be picked from the bus station. This was done before retiring home. By then I was tired, hungry and confused.

I had agreed with the doctors that I was to return to the hospital around 8 a.m. the following morning so that we could map the way forward, including possible transfer to a better equipped hospital. No doubt the night was sleepless for me. Around 6 a.m. on 3 December 2007, I was caught in a deep slumber and I saw Rose in a dream walking towards me. I could clearly see her lower legs.

"How is it that you can walk freely without the aid of crutches and without any cast or bandages on your legs after such a horrific accident?" I asked.

She smiled. "I have been healed and have no need for such apparatus," was her response.

As it turned out, that must have been the time she was struggling with her soul and it was her way of telling me that the wounds were no longer of any consequence to her as she was now entering another world. The new Rose did not need the broken limbs as fresh ones had been supplied.

Suffice it to mention that the majority of my dreams are always fictitious with fictitious characters. Rarely do I dream of people that I know and real events as in this instance. I can only surmise that she was actually communicating with me to the effect that she was no longer a physical being but a spiritual one.

At exactly 8 a.m. I was at the hospital with her toiletries and night dress. The senior nursing sister on duty advised me that Rose's condition had remained stable and that the doctors were then undertaking their morning rounds and when they were through they would confer with me on the next move. I had no reason to suspect that anything unpleasant could have transpired. What surprised me was that there was quite a crowd of doctors and nurses at Rose's bedside and wondered why there would be so many at the same time, when other patients had none. The sister took the toiletries and advised me she would wash Rose up and once that was done she would call me so that I could see her although it was not official visiting time. I waited until about 9.30a.m. when two senior doctors and two sisters came into the room where I had been waiting for what appeared to have been eternity. I expected them to give me the report I had been waiting for. I however noticed that they all wore gloomy faces although at that time I didn't suspect anything untoward. One of them then said, "We are sorry that we failed to resuscitate your wife."

That did not make any sense to me because no one had earlier mentioned any need for resuscitation to me. All I knew was that I was waiting to see my wife and to be given the report on her condition, having been assured earlier that her condition had been stable overnight. He then clarified,

"When the sister tried to sit her up so that she could be bathed, your wife just collapsed and all subsequent efforts to resuscitate her failed," the doctor continued.

"Are you telling me that my wife is gone?" I asked.

"Yes Mr. Matutu. We tried our best. We are really sorry."

I sat there, motionless and confused. My mind went completely blank. 'Was I dreaming', I wondered? 'No, this was real,' I assured myself. I sat there, looking at them, numb with shock and disbelief, not knowing what to do or say. I felt empty. Life became meaningless. Even though I started to cry and fell to the ground when reality had sunk, I had still not fully comprehended the situation. I still had a lot of tasks ahead of me that afternoon and evening. It was only when people started arriving home to pay their condolences that I fully acknowledged my predicament (see next chapter).

I suspect that blood, which may have coagulated to some extent, must have rushed to her heart as they made her to sit up and a blood clot may have rushed and blocked one of the passages in the heart. Remember, she already had a problem with deep vein thrombosis.

By this time I was all alone, with Lazarus having once again gone to look for *Gogo MaNcube* whom he could not find once more (she had already left for the hospital). The doctors advised that my wife had died of excessive bleeding.

"Why did you not mention that she had bled excessively yesterday? Why is it that her deep shin wound had not been bleeding? Also, why was there was no indication of excessive blood in the car or anywhere near the area of the accident?" I asked.

"I cannot quite explain that except to confirm that she had very little blood left in her by the time she died," the doctor replied.

"If she had lost that much blood why was there no blood transfusion ordered for her yesterday?" I continued to probe.

"We were still in the process of establishing her blood group and in any case the intravenous drip that we administered had some blood in it," was the response.

I was not satisfied but saw the futility of further debate. 'I have a job and God is in control,' I told myself.

Time of death was reported as 9:10 a.m. although she may have been struggling when I arrived, hence the large contingent of medical staff around her bed. I therefore strongly doubt that I was told the truth on my arrival, not that it would have made any difference. The post mortem would later confirm cause of death as excessive internal bleeding and the splintered femur.

This explained why there had been minimal bleeding through the deep cut in the shin as most of the blood had collected internally. I would like to believe that if the hospital had had top of the range medical equipment, the internal injuries and bleeding could have been detected earlier and possible corrective action taken in time.

Meanwhile, Lazarus had returned without *Gogo* and we had to wait until she pitched up with Aunt Mrs. Mtisi and Aunt Mrs. Khoza around the visiting time of 1 p.m. He was also devastated with the news. All this time the senior sister was with us. In the interim I had to gather courage and started phoning our children who are all based abroad as well as friends and relatives.

What had transpired the previous day was that when Rose had reached the civic centre along Harare Drive in Marlborough (suburb), on her way home from Kuwadzana, at around 9:30 a.m., she most likely fell asleep from fatigue due to lack of sleep as has already been mentioned. She simply left her side of the road at what appeared to be excessive speed and rammed into an Isuzu pickup coming from the opposite direction. The acceleration appeared to be consistent with someone asleep as her foot would have been flat on the fuel pedal. The force was so intense that the driver's cabin was shattered and heavily compressed. The steering wheel must have pushed into her chest with massive force resulting in the wheel being crumbled to a little ball of twisted metal. Unfortunately, the car was not equipped with airbags. On-lookers and worshippers from a nearby Catholic Church quickly came to her rescue but struggled to extricate her from the cramped cabin. Ambulances and the police were quickly summoned. As she was unconscious no one could identify her and notify her next of kin.

While all this was happening, I was sitting in the church pew oblivious of the unfolding tragedy. By the time she was evacuated it was 11:10 a.m., one hour and forty minutes later, and to this day I have never got a satisfactory explanation of how this huge time lag arose.

One of the explanations was that the ambulance team had demanded that their fees be paid prior to evacuation, only succumbing later to pressure from the onlookers. She was then taken to a private hospital where staff there also demanded cash payment of fees prior to admission. This practice become a sad development arising from our country's economic meltdown as hospitals risk non-payment of fees if patients are accepted before payment, whatever the condition of the patient. She was finally taken to Parirenyatwa Government Hospital as there was no one to make the payment. By that time two hours had elapsed from time of accident and clearly this delay contributed significantly to her demise. As fate would have it, with the flat battery on her mobile telephone and all her personal papers having been placed in the boot of the vehicle, no one was able to track down any of her relatives or acquaintances. She was simply an individual without identity.

The above narrative is what I found out after I left hospital but the real truth appears to have eluded me as I don't know for sure if she slept on the steering wheel and why it took so long for the medical staff to take her to hospital. In the final analysis, the fact is that she is gone and no amount of detail on how it happened will help bring her back. Although I managed to contact the driver of the other vehicle, it was of little help as she appeared to be more interested in defending herself rather than objectively narrate how the accident had occurred. It has therefore not been my priority to pursue the matter with her any further.

The ambulance team that evacuated her from the accident scene incidentally belongs to a subsidiary company of Rose's employers. They insisted that they arrived at the scene immediately after the accident and that to the best of their knowledge, they did not contribute to any delays. I have also decided not to pursue matter further.

At about the time of accident, Mrs. Madziwa, a friend of Rose's, had a unique experience while seated in a church pew. Although they were not very close friends there was a special connection between these two ladies. Mrs. Madziwa has a son with the Down's syndrome, who had developed a special bond with Rose for many years. Whenever he saw Rose he would be very excited and happy. At the time of accident, Mrs. Madziwa started to feel some excruciating pain in her legs. It was so unbearable that she had to be rushed to hospital by ambulance. The x-rays taken proved negative and she was kept there for observation but nothing else has been found to this day. I cannot say for certain that the two incidences were connected but I felt it intriguing and worth mentioning. Incidentally, Rose's research paper on her degree program focused on children with Down's syndrome. She must have been thinking of this boy a lot during the preceding weeks and probably at the time of the accident as she had just driven past the Madziwa home.

This is how Rose's life ended on this wretched earth: a life that had touched many people in different walks of life. Hers had been a selfless life which many people had not appreciated, not because she was too sophisticated and distant but because she was simple, loving and accommodating. Not even I, as her husband, had fully understood her and expecting others to have done so would be unrealistic of me. How I now wish I had spent her last night by her bedside. Not that it would have made any difference but at least it would have been a symbolic token of appreciation for her unwavering love for me over the years and would have given me an opportunity to share her last moments on earth with her. That's the least she deserved. Although I know that there was little I could have done to save her life, one cannot help but have that lingering feeling that something could have been done to change the course of events. There was certainly a serious lack of judgment from both of us in that she should never have driven in the condition she was in and I should have probably skipped church to attend to the errands. I know however, that altering the course of events would not have changed her fate as it had already been sealed. I take comfort in that she is up there with our Lord Jesus, whom she served tirelessly, for she feared God and strove to serve him whatever the circumstances.

The wisest man who ever lived, King Solomon of the nation of Israel sums it up in his book, Ecclesiastes, by saying everything is meaningless. He says that it doesn't matter what one achieves or does in this life, it all ends in death. This fate visits the powerful and the oppressed, the rich and the poor, the wise and the foolish. He concludes by saying that the crux of the matter is for us to fear God and obey his commands, for that is our all (all we are here for). (Ecclesiastes 12:13).

Reference passages; Eccl 12:13, 1 Chr 16:30, Psalm 2:11, Prov 1:7, Matt 10:28, Luke 1:50, Eph 5:21, 1 Peter 1:17 and Rev 14:7

# 19

## The Funeral Wake and Grieving

*We often suffer because we tend to focus on the body. A human being is made of the soul and the body. We should allow our souls unfettered freedom to communicate with God and that way provide relief for the body.*

Storms come, mostly unexpected, and leave trails of havoc and destruction. They destroy all types of nature, both animate and inanimate. They are always unwelcome yet they play a vital role in the ecosystem. When life is destroyed, the bereaved cries bitterly, yet with time, another type of life begins. However, it is most difficult, in fact impossible, for the bereaved to be optimistic under such circumstances, yet God always provides the answer and is always there to comfort us and always true to his word. Despite this assurance, I grieved a lot and am still grieving.

The hours immediately following the sad moment, were by far the most confusing, yet hectic, for me. I had to cope with the reality of the sudden loss and the related shock while at the same time I had to personally inform relatives and friends. Advising the children, was the most difficult part. A few hours earlier I had advised them that mother had been involved in a road traffic accident and badly hurt although doctors had assured us that the worst was over. Now I had to tell them the dreaded news. I managed to phone Tatenda and Fadzi who informed the others but the crying over the phone was difficult to manage, what with me in a similarly helpless state, no one could comfort the other. By evening there was a huge gathering, mainly from church members. Fadzi, Lynda, Kevin and Simba all arrived on Wednesday, December 5, given their ten hours time saving. Tatenda and Munya arrived on Friday, losing time in their eastwards flight, having insisted that burial be delayed until their arrival. I had earlier on arranged for burial on Friday so that the mourners could be released to their homes but when Tatenda insisted that he wanted to witness everything I relented. I had to consider the possible negative feelings that could have lingered on in his life just because of the saving of one day.

Relatives and friends continued to arrive from various parts of the country and abroad, mainly Botswana and Zambia. Neighbours streamed in. Her employers were represented at very senior level and contributed generously towards the funeral related expenses. The church arranged for daily evening worship services as is the norm. Donations in cash and kind were received from various corners. Special mention has to be made of our church friends, Jefta and Tsitsi Mugweni who donated a cow for meat as well as vegetables which were fully appreciated. Despite the huge crowd, the meat was more than adequate.

Grieving was by far the most difficult part. At first I was confused, as if I was dreaming. Many a times we see our friends losing their loved ones and we rush to console them. That is well and good. However, I never appreciated how devastating it was for them until it happened to me. It would be trite for me to recount here how wonderful my mother was as there have been countless renditions on mother's love and how wonderful mothers are in general. Suffice it to say that mother was no exception. I was therefore devastated when she passed on in 2002 as she was very special to me. While we have no choice of who our mothers are, we have millions of choices of who we choose for a wife. I now realise that in my case, it was not a choice, but a gift from God. Therefore, her departure was far much more devastating than I had ever experienced.

The other reason I took a severe knock when Rose left me was whereas my bonding with mother had somehow been interrupted by my leaving home early, first for boarding school and later for work at a young age, I had lived with Rose for a good thirty years. These were years of love… of sharing…of happiness… of frustrations. What I cherished most was the love and the sharing; sharing the big and the small things… the good and the bad…the trivial and the important…sharing everything. We shared food and we shared stories and experiences. We shared our bodies. Although I did not realise it then, the best thing we ever shared was our faith in Jesus and God. It is this faith that is now carrying me through the darkest moments of my life. That is what made the difference between the bonding I had with Rose and the one I had with mother; the former being at a higher level. Ultimately it was this level of bonding that determined the size of the void left in my life. When God says that when two are married they become one flesh, it is a fact. A physical part of me is now down there in the grave with my beloved wife. I take comfort that it is only the physical part of her and not the soul that is down there. While the flesh is hurting I can still relate to her spirit. Her values had become my values and her God, my God.

Those dreams of huge gatherings that I had have become a reality, fulfilled. 'If there is some power out there which reveals these things to me before they happen, why does this same power not reveal more so that I can understand issues better or clearer? Why bombard me with riddles and leave me puzzled? Why not the full story? Why the bits and pieces? Even if I got the full story, what would I do with it anyway? Nothing, virtually nothing, for I am only but human with so many things well beyond me. The world of the spirit is only but a mirage for me, never to be realised until my time comes. Then, only then, will I be able to understand. It will be too late to save the living. O God, I am toiling under this infirmity…this handicap… please relieve me.'

For now, I only understand in part; then I shall understand in full, just to borrow the words of Apostle Paul when writing about love in 1 Corinthians 13:12.

## Why her?
Death is the ultimate price anyone can ever pay. We all can understand less final misfortunes but this. Why didn't she live with infirmities like many others do? The mere thought that she is no more is mind boggling. Is she really gone; non existent? Was it anything wrong she had done? What became of all that gentleness and courteousness; the kindness? Is there anything I could have done to prevent it or that I can do to bring her back? All these are just hopeless thoughts racing through my mind. Given what I have already written about Rose, the human part of me wonders why she was taken at that specific time. Why would God take someone of such beauty and strength of character? Had she done enough of her good works? Why did God not prevent this? Yet the spiritual part of me knows better. Death is not an end but the beginning of new things. Just like a seed that has to die so that a plant may sprout and bear fruits. Just like Christ had to die so that we could live, those who die in the Lord shall surely live, for now they are just asleep. For that reason I am certain that she is in heaven right now. She is in excellent company, the company

that many of us may strive for but never attain. Even those who attain it, they only do so by the creator's grace.

## Why me?

Why has God dealt so harshly with me? Is God punishing me for my commissions and omissions? Since he had favoured me with Rose's companionship for a good thirty years, what has changed now? Does God still love me or has he forsaken me? Did I in any way contribute towards this unwelcome event? Is it my fault? What has gone wrong? All answers are beyond my reach. Strange as it may sound, I know Rose is lucky to have been taken when her faith was so strong and that she has already gone through that gate she was singing of. However, it would appear that I am the one being punished for I am in serious torment right now while she is comfortable in God's arms. Only in good time will I be able to understand the full picture. Ultimately, I don't cry for my wife but for myself! It's me who has lost the comfort of her companionship which I badly need right now while on the other hand, she doesn't need me any more! She has far much better company and is celebrating full time. God willing, I will join them when my time comes. For now I am confined inside this wretched body and its infirmities... trapped...a prisoner.

## Why now?

Why did this happen at this stage in our lives? I am in semi retirement looking forward to new challenges in life while she was looking at completing her degree program. My eyes were set on establishing a consulting and training firm focusing on the banking industry as well as a bit of horticultural farming at my small plot in Chegutu. We were now also looking at all our children completing their university programs as well, and with Tatenda already married, we were looking forward to be grandparents one of these days, God willing. Despite some marital problems earlier on in our relationship, matters were generally going well for us. Our spiritual life was also at what I would call reasonable level. Then this disaster! All I can say is; "My God, why now?"

## What next?

How will I face tomorrow? What do I do with the physical gap in my life? How do I guide the children alone? How will I face all the evidence of her prior existence, both in my life in particular and in the home in general? I cannot just pretend that she never existed as evidence is everywhere and overwhelming. Her influence on my own grooming and that of the children is also very evident. There is no way we would have all turned out to be what we are today without her input. I simply cannot imagine life without my Rose although I will have to move on, although I don't know where to. I am sure it is not a case of me appreciating my water after the well has run dry.

Clearly, there is only one answer to all these questions: God knows what is better for me; he is in charge and cannot be questioned. He is not answerable to anyone. Interestingly, I am no longer afraid of death. This experience has taught me that it is only those who remain behind who are tormented. The departed are oblivious of the wretchedness of death, for death has become a nonentity...irrelevant.

## The children

I need to commend my children, including my *muroora*, for the way they conducted themselves during the difficult period. None of them had ever experienced the death of a close relative, let alone one as close as a mother. They were obviously devastated when they heard of the news but by the time they arrived, they had somewhat accepted that mum was gone. On arrival, they were all overwhelmed, both by being in the presence of mourners and by the sheer numbers of people. Thanks to the elders of the church who grouped themselves into welcoming parties for receiving the children at the airport. In Zimbabwean culture, crying is a generally discouraged practice although I think mourning should be an exception. It was Kevin, as usual, who first voiced his concern to me that everyone was rushing to discourage him from crying for his mum and that he took great exception to that. He asked why he was not allowed to grieve for his mother. In closed discussions with him and his siblings, we all agreed with him, but I had to explain the rationale and apologized for the practice. Otherwise, I fully agree that people should be allowed to cry or even wail for their beloved ones as their emotions dictate and that, we Zimbabweans should change this part of our tradition. Crying is a natural way of letting out emotion and should be encouraged when appropriate.

*     *     *

When writing Psalm 8, David wondered why God loved man so much that he made man a little lower than the angels and gave him dominion over all earthly living creatures. Yet, when compared with the rest of God's creation like the universe, man appears insignificant, at least in stature. Although I am aware of this assurance, the human part of me tends to take control of me for now. I hurt so much that my body is numb. I pray that God may forgive me for my little faith.

I am however encouraged because I have no doubt that Rose is not dead. She has simply left this world for a better one. In fact, she has conquered death, for death has no hold over her anymore and can never visit her again. Her role on earth has been completed and she has heeded the roll call for the best of worlds. I always visualize that infectious laugh of hers as she celebrates her moments of rapture with the other saints up there. I can imagine her saying, excitedly in her newly acquired heavenly language;

"I have made it, that you Lord Jesus for your death on that cross!"

How I now look forward to that glorious day. Whereas I was despondent and confused soon after her departure, I am now stronger and not scared of my own death anymore. The only reason I would not like to leave now is my children who I know would be devastated should that happen. It is bad enough to lose one parent, losing both is something else. For me, it is irrelevant whether I live or leave now. I am further comforted in that God has always been gracious to me despite my sins and I am convinced he will continue to do so. Therefore, whether I live or leave is entirely his prerogative. Truly, I am not scared of either option. Not that I am perfect but that I am imperfect...not that I am righteous but that God is gracious...for by myself I am but nothing, simply nothing.

Even as I periodically visit Rose's grave to place her favourite white roses, it is only to sooth my emotions. It is not for her benefit. The truth is that what is down there in the ground is not Rose but her bones (the flesh has already disappeared) because my Rose is in a place too beautiful to be comprehended by human mind. Her date of departure from this earth, December 3, 2007 is her birthday into a better life... a day I will always cherish. It has just dawned on me that when we celebrate our earthly birthdays, we are celebrating our imminent departure from this world and the advent of a new, eternal birthday. That should be the focus of our celebrations... the future and not the past...the past is sunk and gone...never to return. We should therefore look forward to that day with hope and not with foreboding and trepidation.

Even as I shall arrange for a beautiful tombstone for Rose's grave, it will be for my satisfaction, for it will be totally irrelevant to her… for things of this earth are no longer of relevance to her but to us the living.

Reference passages;
1. Job 1:21, Psalm 49:15, Psalm 116:15, Eccl 4:2, Rom 14:7, 1 Cor 15:55-57, Phil 1:21, 1 Thes 4:13-14, Rev 14:13
2. Job 19: 25, Luke 12:27, 2 Tim 4:2, 2 Tim 4: 6-8, 1 Peter 1:7, 1 Peter 4:13, 1 Peter 5:4, Rev 3:11, and Rev 16:15

# 20

## More Premonitions

*We are what we are not because we are clever, but because we have a destiny.*

While the twitching of the eye stopped immediately the day Rose passed on, to my bewilderment and confusion, the unwelcome portentous dreams continued unabated, as frequently as before her departure. To say that I was confused and worried is an understatement; I was simply helpless, a prisoner of some powerful visiting forces whose objective was beyond me.

'Surely, not again' I cried to God. 'Who is the next in line and how soon? Will I survive another family death so soon after this one? Will it strike within my immediate family once again? What is this power that reveals these things to me and for what purpose? What am I supposed to do with the knowledge? Who am I to have such things revealed to me?' I continued to ponder.

I also started recording these dreams in my daily diary and shared these with my family and the church elders on a regular basis. For two Sundays in a row when I shared with the church, I failed to control myself with emotion and ended up crying.

In my confusion and moment of need, I suddenly remembered that God would provide an answer and started praying fervently, asking God to deliver me from whatever calamity that could have been lurking. I had never thought that one could pray for God to prevent death, but I did and God did not disappoint me. As already been mentioned, in most of my dreams I see a gathering of relatives in an obvious funeral environment. But when I started praying, there was a clear change in how these dreams were concluded. An escape route suddenly became a feature at the end of such dreams. The dreams always came just before I got up in the morning, probably deliberately so that I could remember them with ease. One morning I dreamt the usual funeral crowd. Towards the end, I was sent on an assignment but on my return someone told me to avoid the crowd. Somehow I found myself driving a motor vehicle with which I took a detour and avoided the crowd and got away. When the crowd realized what had happened, they pursued me. To my relief, immediately after I went past a certain spot, the police arrived and set up a road block. When my pursuers came along they were denied passage and I thus made my escape good.

Upon waking up, I clearly realized that God had answered my prayers and thanked him. I shared this with my sister in Christ, *Thulani* Sibanda when she visited in the morning to comfort me. That evening, I received a call from my young brother, Philemon's son, *Tinashe* advising that his father had been admitted in a Marondera hospital with an extremely high blood pressure that measured 220/160 on the monitor. In many instances, that level of blood pressure would result in a stroke, leaving the victim possibly paralyzed, or at worst would be fatal. Immediately, I took this as confirmation that God had indeed answered my prayers; otherwise there was no explanation of how Philemon had survived that situation. On enquiry, I was advised that he had not taken his medication for two days after it had run out. He could not visit the doctor for replenishment because he had been too busy at work. He is a manager at a local bank and the month had been a terribly busy one for banks as they were failing to meet their clients' cash requirements. That could have also exacerbated the blood pressure.

I also suspect that he may not have been taking his medication deliberately. He and his wife belong to a Pentecostal church that makes them believe that such a condition can be cured through prayer. I strongly remonstrated with the two and told them that if this was the case, their conduct was uncalled for and that they were putting him at serious risk. My own health was also at risk as head of the greater family as I simply could not face another death. **Not that I doubt that God answers prayers and can heal; He has just done that for me.** What I do not agree with is that we should test God with what is clearly a life threatening condition to the total exclusion of his very gift to us of modern medicine. It is akin to one lying down on a busy highway and praying that God saves him from passing traffic! The gigantic strides made by mankind in medicine and other spheres of science over the past few decades can only be attributable to God who is the source of all knowledge and wisdom, for on his own, man is unable to attain such heights.

While God may withhold his healing blessings whenever he sees fit, for me the answer was swift and positive, even a prayer against death. How I wish I had prayed likewise for my dear wife, she would probably be with me today.

I immediately thanked God for prayers answered and I continue to do so to this day. Further dreams were to follow with almost all of them having escape routes and eventually they stopped. However, let me share with you just one more of these fascinating dreams. I dreamt that I had just bought a bus which I was driving and had stopped at shopping centre when a number of people invited themselves for a ride into town. The police tried to block my passage on the charge that I had no licence to carry passengers. After long negotiations, they allowed me to proceed with the passengers. I came across a bridge on the Mupete River, ten kilometres away from Zvishavane town on the Gweru highway. The bridge had been swept away by the flooded river but I managed to negotiate the bus through the sandy and bumpy river bed. When I thought I had succeeded, I came across a toll gate where once again I negotiated the bus through an extremely narrow space which left everyone who watched in amazement. When I woke up, I once again thanked God for providing me with yet another escape. To my utter amazement and bewilderment, exactly two months later, it was announced on national radio and television that that very bridge had been swept away by the flooded Mupete River. I had occasion to visit the bridge before it was repaired and witnessed it for myself. Indeed, passage was through the sandy riverbed. Of interest is that the water that swept this bridge away drains my village where the river has its source in the Mbirashava Mountains where I grew up herding cattle. To this day, I have no clear explanation as to why such things would be revealed to me and the purpose thereof.

One morning after that dream, I heard a loud voice in yet another dream telling me that if I needed more revelations, I should simply ask for them and they would be revealed to me. My daughter Lynda also heard a similar voice telling her that if she thought this was heavy, worse things were to follow. Although I don't fully understand the purpose and full meaning of such phenomena, I cannot reject these revelations outright and I have accordingly prayed that when similar occurrences are revealed to me in future, they be accompanied by a full clarification. It is the confusion that is unwelcome. Meanwhile I continue to pray that God may deliver me from any further deaths that may still be lurking out there. I have no doubt that he will deliver me.

The instant answers to my prayers concerning my dreams in general and the one relating to Philemon in particular have certainly strengthened my faith in God and His providence. There are many instances in the Bible where God's people prayed and got instant relief from Him. He also appeared to have saved my family from what appeared to have been imminent catastrophe, the nature of which I have no idea.

Two more occurrences were to come as surprises for me. Firstly, I met the deadline date by which my publishers expected me to submit the manuscript of this book and to make a down payment of the fees if I was to benefit from some discounts. This was 30 November 2008, three days before the first anniversary of Rose's departure! Secondly, Tatenda, who had exhausted all his leave days found himself booked for leave on the anniversary of his mother's departure. It is not clear who authorised that leave and when it was done. Was this by divine providence? I don't know.

Reference passages;
1. Gen 18:23-33. Judges 6:36-40. 1 Sam 1:1-18. Matt 8:2-3. Matt 8:5-13. Acts 9:40
2. Isa 38:21, Jer 8:22, Jer 30:13,zek 47:12, Matt 9:12, Col 4:14, Rev 22:2
3. 2 Cor 12:7-9, 1 Tim 5:23

# 21

# Coping

*There are times when excessive pain is better than no pain at all, for one who has gone through such an experience can only be wiser than the one who has not.*

Yes, I went through a lot of pain...emotional pain...like I had never experienced. It is this experience, though supposedly negative, that has galvanized me against adversity and made me to appreciate God more. I pray that when and if a similar occurrence arises, I should be able to accept God's hand in it and not to question him.

Misfortunes always befall man and although at times the situation looks hopeless, there is usually a way out. Unfortunately, death is a misfortune of its own kind, the ultimate misfortune to befall mortal man. While for the dead faithful there is a way out, for the unbeliever there is no salvation except by the grace of God. In both cases, coping for the remaining family can therefore be a devastating and traumatic experience. While no one can claim experience on mourning, for every death touches us differently, we learn to know that God is in total control; hence the wisdom after the pain. Therefore, the impact is always manageable when we surrender everything to God, for he always reveals his purpose to us. It has taken the death of a loved one for many of us to realize the futility of our ways and to turn to God during the bereaving period. I would like to thank God that by the time of her departure, Rose had brought my children and me to his fold. Notwithstanding her human blemishes, she had lived an exemplary life that we should endeavour to emulate. Coping has therefore not been as traumatic as I had expected despite the pain. This is because we have HOPE although I always pray that my hope be increased.

The following activities contributed in their different ways in helping me to cope.

## Refocusing on God

First and foremost, I had to turn to God for an answer. There were moments when I felt let down and somewhat frustrated with God. I then realized that God cannot be put on a pedestal for questioning for he is the Alpha and the Omega. Without him there was nothing…there is nothing and there will be nothing. I then fully submitted myself to him and that is how I managed the subsequent premonitions which I take to be a form of communication from him. That is when I started praying earnestly and I was not disappointed with the results.

## Crying

I cried a lot during and after the wake. Although I may have appeared to be strong on burial day, I often cried when recounting the story of my wife and her impact on my life. I decided to defy the norm by refusing to bottle my emotions in. Crying is a natural process that should be allowed to take its course. Likewise, while the presence of the extended family is greatly appreciated during grieving, they tend to distract one from focussing on the matter at hand. Grieving is thus suppressed and like crying, will only resurface later, by which time one should have moved on. There is an effect of postponing the inevitable.

## Writing this book

The idea of writing this book came to me before we buried my dear wife when I completed the first draft outline. The writing process has provided a lot of comfort as I often went back memory lane recalling the early days of our lives, both the good and the bad. A significant part of my time was consumed by the writing which has helped me to focus. Of note is that a number of sentences in this book were constructed not only whilst in bed but fast asleep, in my dreams! I remember debating one sentence with someone in a dream and waking up remembering it very clearly.

## The Funeral service

Without any forethought, I found Tatenda and myself leading the casket into the church building for service ahead of the undertaker. As the last person to view the body before burial, I had the privilege of shutting the casket for the last time, once again this was not planned. I cherish that moment...it is befitting that I was the last person to see her body before it was laid to rest. Though somewhat dramatic, whenever I recall these two incidences, they help me to accept that Rose has indeed gone. Imagine the difference if I had sat somewhere in the background only to hear that she had been buried. This would leave me with some hazy picture of the incidence. In this context, Tatenda's request that we await his and Munya's arrival before the burial clears makes sense. I was also greatly encouraged as I listened to my children speak fondly of their mother.

## Gardening

I mentioned earlier the devotion that Rose had to her plants and flowers. She would often call me to join her in admiring a plant when I was resting on the couch after a taxing game of golf. I now remember her by taking time to water these plants and often by walking among them. Initially it made me cry but now I often wonder how she would have remarked on seeing how beautiful some of the plants have become. No doubt, she knew how most of them would look like at full maturity. Of particular interest is one big orchid that was in full bloom at time of writing. It shows that Rose had mastered the art of growing orchids as they are not easy to grow.

## Family photograph albums

I have spent countless times going through the family photo albums which include Rose's as a maiden and those as a young mother of our children. I have shared these pictured several times with those visiting me. I have even gone though the gruesome burial photographs which initially gave me shivers. I have since scanned the majority of these on to my lap top where they also function as the screensaver.

## Children

My children, including my *muroora*, played a big role in my recovery. They went out of their way to encourage me by word of mouth and by deed. It was as if I had lost more than they had. They appeared to have recovered faster than me although I know some of them struggled when they returned to their bases abroad and are still hurting. They also continued to send me emails of encouragement which I cherished a lot. Whilst my children are obviously not the best in the world, for they have their own faults, I am proud of what they have turned out to be. My mother used to tell of how grateful she was that all her children had turned out to be what they were, no matter how modest, and how all credit should not be hers but be given to God.

"**For humans, in their own right, are unable to determine the ultimate character of their offspring unless God desires it,**" **she would reason.**

## Church and friends

The church was extremely supportive during the seven day wake with many running around with many errands including picking the children from the airport and provision of the various forms of food. After the burial, I broke down on two consecutive Sundays indicating that I grieved more then than during the wake and burial. It must have been clear to many that I was in need of more consoling. A number of church members continued to visit and console me. That is as it should be. However, I had expected many more such visits, particularly soon after the burial.

## Screensaver

I turned one of Rose's recent photographs into the screen background of my laptop and mobile phone so that I see her every time I switch these gadgets on. Initially, it was hard but with time, I got used.

## Further premonitions

After the burial I received further premonitions which I shared with the family and the church. At first I was overwhelmed and didn't know what to do as the premonitions became a continued source of worry and anxiety. At a time when I was clearly desperate and somewhat directionless, prayer and guidance from God became my source of comfort...I was able to overcome. The negatives suddenly turned into positives and my life changed for the better. Where there was despair, there is hope.

## Testimonies

The testimonies were a huge source of comfort and inspiration for me. Knowing how Rose had assisted many people, even strangers, and having these come to her funeral and giving their testimonies was a humbling and encouraging experience for me. I was certainly encouraged to move on. That is when I first had the idea of writing this book.

## Bedtime

By default, I have always slept on the side of our matrimonial bed nearest the door or furthest from the wall of our bedroom. This has been consistent despite the number of bedrooms we have occupied over the thirty years of our marriage. By default, this was designed in such a way that Rose would be protected from any intruders that may come. Since her departure, I have had occasion to sleep on her side of the bed. This somehow helps me to minimize the void that would otherwise be too gaping for comfort. It is also like a reflex rearranging of the bed so that things are no longer in their original place; for she is indeed no longer occupying that place. Of course, I still miss my Rose despite these efforts.

\*     \*     \*

By no means have these measures taken away the pain; to the contrary, there are times when going through them pains so much that I can hardly bear it. At times I doubt if I am doing the right thing. However, in the final analysis, the pain is eased through the soothing experience of the regular exposures. That way these measures have significantly helped me to soldier on, hard as it has been. I trust that the pain that I have gone through will leave me a better person spiritually and any otherwise. At the time of writing, I still cried whenever I gave or heard testimony on my dear departed one. I am reminded of the story of a man who had experienced lots and lots of misfortunes, more or less like Job had. He took his heavy load to God and pleaded with him to have the load exchanged for a lighter one. The man was invited to surrender his burden and to go into the Room of Burdens and to select the burden of his choice. As he went around the room, he got excited as he picked the smallest packet from among some gigantic ones. Suddenly, he heard a voice saying to him;

"Well done my son, you have taken back your load."

It is God alone who knows the size and type of the burden that I am able to carry despite any notions I may have.

\*     \*     \*

Whoever said God was not logical? On 28 May 1952, a soul descended from heaven and was given a perishable body and became a male human being, with all its imperfections. Likewise, on 1 March 1953, another beautiful soul became a female human being. In his wisdom God bonded these two into one flesh in 1977. With God as the main architect, the two started constructing a beautiful nest. In due time, he enhanced the beauty of that nest with the addition of four lovely offspring and the nest was thus fully inhabited. Whilst the two were still enjoying this beauty and companionship, in no time the nest started to get empty by virtue of departing offspring, slowly but surely, culminating with the last departure in February 2006, and leaving the two original occupants, behind…just as they had begun. Sure, who would have minded as long as the two remained as one? Then, in a flash, the one flesh became half! On 3 December 2007, one of the souls returned to its permanent place of abode, leaving the perishable tent behind to decay. The perishable and the imperishable had once again been separated. The reversal process had gathered momentum; the nest was fast disintegrating, leaving the remaining half exposed to the elements. How long it will hold before total disintegration, only the good Lord knows. For now, only a rudimental structure of the once splendid nest remains. Thank you Lord. I truly thank you for the privilege of having known this beautiful soul. (*Makaita henyu Ishe, makaita zvirokwazvo)'.*

But when I am physically alone at home, there are times when the emptiness of the nest overwhelms me. I simply cannot fathom it. However, I always resort to the assurance that even in adversity, God is indeed wonderful, for I know that at least I am not alone and that assurance is enough to make me pull through. Psalm 23 becomes very relevant, for indeed there is no need for me to fear any evil, for God has always been with me and there is no reason why he should leave me alone now.

May the Almighty be praised for giving us the gift of forgetfulness, for in due time, I shall forget the pain; if not in full, at least in part.

Reference passages; 2 Peter 1:12-15, Psalm 23, Psalm 8

# 22

## The Legacy

*As stubborn as the truth: one can always twist and stretch lies without limit but the truth will always remain stubbornly unmoved.*

It is this stubbornness that gives the truth its unique character; the character that brings us closer to God. If there are any untruths contained in this book, they are not intentional and will in no way affect the personality of my departed Rose, for that has already been cast in stone and may neither be stretched nor moved. Who Rose Sibusisiwe Matutu really was will always remain a stubborn fact which can neither be twisted nor stretched. She strove to live an honest life, a selfless life denominated by love for God and for others as defined by her works.

No doubt Rose has left an indelible mark in the Matutu family and its acquaintances. She has set such lofty standards that it would be next to impossible for mere mortals to emulate her, yet it can be done. The challenges come in that Rose did not appear to have acquired these virtues over time, nor were they acquired of human effort. They appear to have been inborn. How then does one attain such heights unless they are given to one by the grace of God? She has thrown the gauntlet and no one appears to be ready to pick it up, yet

As head of family, the challenge is more for me than it is for anyone else. It is only I who can carry the torch and ensure everyone sees the light and I pray that God may grant me courage and that he may spare my life a little longer so that I may do his will. On my part, I accept the challenge.

One interesting thing with Rose was that she was not well read, neither in secular matters nor those of faith. Her knowledge was therefore limited to either what she had read academically or observed in life. She always remarked at what she considered to be my wide general knowledge and wondered how and when I had acquired it during the thirty years of our companionship. I am generally a good observer of nature and easily assimilate some issues many would consider irrelevant. To that extent, I have been a member of the winning teams many times over in the annual inter banks quiz competitions in Zimbabwe. I also conduct the annual Bible quiz at Avondale Church of Christ. The import of this point is to show that knowledge, even of the Bible, is not necessarily a requisite for one to be a better Christian. It is my considered view that Rose was by far a better Christian than I and for this I give credit to God and to *Gogo MaNdlovu*, her childhood mentor. Over the past few years, she had gone out of her way to attend almost all ladies meetings and conferences whenever possible. Accordingly, she has left a number of Bible based booklets and notes on how to be a better Christian. Suddenly, she had become an avid reader of the Bible, possibly in preparation for her departure for the celestial city: a city where pain and sorrow are unwelcome aliens, a city where there is no night.

There will be no excuse whatsoever for me and the children to go astray as the bar has been set. It is my prayer that all future generations may know Him from whom all life originates and flows. Pretending that any one of us is in charge of our lives can only be ridiculous and foolish.

Reference passages; 1 Cor 13, 1 John 4: 20-21, 2 Tim 1: 12.

# SECTION THREE

## REFLECTIONS

# 23

# Special Letters

*Without communication, we are groping in the dark, in circles.*

It was my good friend and brother in Christ, that affable and scholarly gentleman, Eubert Mashaire, who suggested that I write a special letter to my departed wife as part of the grieving and healing process. He had noticed how I had struggled to adjust after I had gone up to the pulpit on two occasions to express my gratitude to the church only to end up narrating my problems and crying. He then consulted a psychologist friend of his who suggested this therapy. I must say that it did help a lot and thanks a lot, my brother.

I have since decided to include a number of letters in this chapter including letters One and Two which I wrote to Rose in 2006 following our disagreement on Kwazi after I had suggested that the latter come home to meet her half siblings during Tatenda and Munyaradzi's wedding. Also included are letters from our children. I am very much aware that she is in another world... a better world...and will neither read nor respond to these letters. However these are written in pursuit of the purpose of this book;

to celebrate her life as well as telling her story to the world. They also provide each writer with some form of a relief valve. No doubt, there is a lot of subjectivity in these letters, underlined by emotion.

## 23.1    Letter one

I wrote this letter in pursuit of reconciliation after Rose was angry at me for raising the issue of Kwazi and would not talk to me and had moved out of the matrimonial bedroom to sleep in the adjoining office.

*My Love,*

*All I can say is that I regret not being able to appreciate you for what you are, an honest and caring wife. I have clearly taken you for granted and for that there is no excuse whatsoever. It has taken me too long to appreciate what you really mean to me. I can now see how selfish I have been.*

*I clearly don't deserve the trust and love you have shown me over the years.*

*All I am asking for is your forgiveness this once more.*

*Please give me another chance and I will not let you down. This is my word of honour. I have stopped the arrangement that has offended you and that should not be an issue again. Let me also assure you that I am not having an extra marital relationship.*

*I will also be revising my will shortly and will let you know.*

*In short, please forgive me, give me a chance and I will not let you down again. This    time around, I have learnt my lesson.*

*I cherish you, I cherish your company and I cherish our marriage. Nothing will ever come between us again: at least not from within our union.*

*I know you have no reason to believe me but this promise is not only to you, but to me as well and I intend keeping it. I have now woken up to reality.*

*I will not blame you if you don't accept this plea*

*Your love*

*Bryan.*
*September 4, 2006*

## 23.2    Letter Two

I wrote this letter as follow up to Letter One

*To Rose, my Love*

*For whatever it is worth, let me write again to say I am missing your love very badly. I am missing your company yet you are so near. It pains me to see you in that condition, both for your sake and mine.*

*I am prepared to make this work once and for all. I am therefore prepared to do as you suggest on the matter at any time. We will win if we work together.*

*At the risk of repeating myself, let me say once again that there is no excuse whatsoever for what I did and that I feel so stupid about it all. I had hoped that you would see my point of view.*

*Please don't shut me out of your life, I badly need you. Please let us revert to be that unit of love we so both desire. I will play my part.*

*Bryan*
*September 11, 2006.*

## 23.3   Letter Three

I wrote this letter as part of grieving and healing process after Rose's departure

*To My Love,*
*I know that you will not read this letter as the Bible tells us that the dead know nothing but I hope that somehow, God, in his wisdom, will facilitate this communication or that you will read it on my heart when one day we meet again.*

*My Love, you left me so suddenly and when I least expected it. One of the last vivid memories I have of you was when I collected you from that house in Highfield Township. You greeted me with a very humble face and voice as if you were afraid I would find out you would leave me soon. Why didn't you tell me if you knew? The second one was when you were asleep in the car whilst we waited for the bus at Roadport less than two hours before the accident. How I now wish I had missed church service that morning and allowed you to rest.*

*Let me start by apologizing for all the wrongs I did to you during our life together particularly the issue of infidelity. I know that the birth of a child out of wedlock and the subsequent misunderstandings over her were by far the most hurtful moments for you. I sincerely apologize for that, it was never my intention to deliberately hurt you but rather, a matter of recklessness on my part. Unfortunately, I was unable to make it up to you to your satisfaction until your departure, even though I always tried my best. As you would recall, my view has always been that everyone is entitled to know who their father is and wherever possible, to have normal relations between the two. Please note that since your departure, I have reopened communication with her with a view to normalizing relations between the two of us. I hope that now that you are in the world of the spirits you will be able to appreciate my approach to this issue.*

*I thank God that he gave me an opportunity to share my life with such a wonderful wife; hence I have decided to write this book as tribute to you. I thank you so much for giving me such a wonderful life, for giving me four beautiful children, for your comfort and above all for bringing me to Christ. You were my mother and my provider, my comforter, for thirty good years. There is simply no way the void you have left in my life can be filled by human efforts. Only God can do that.*

*Your love and generosity were without measure, but I scarcely appreciated you when it mattered most. I chose to dwell on our trivial differences. You looked after my family like no other human wife that I know has ever done. Now they are in a latch as no one can ever fill those giant shoes of yours. I have not received any answer as to why it had to be you to lead the way ahead of me. Now I understand it when people say that God only takes the good first, otherwise how would one explain what appears to be such an injustice. It is true that what appears to be foolishness to man is wisdom to God. He certainly knows better. But I take great comfort in knowing that you are in God's beautiful hands.* **"Precious in the sight of the Lord is the death of his saints," Psalms 116 verse 15 tells us.** *I pray that I won't disintegrate for I just don't know who I am anymore or where to start.*

*You worked so hard during the period preceding your departure to the extent that we hardly shared anything outside your school work. Was this a means of weaning me away from you gradually? There was always some activity that separated us although we were never alienated from one another. I know we both had a lot of dreams, the bulk of which we never had an opportunity to share. But you would remember my worrying about some of my dreams after our return from Kwekwe which you brushed aside, maybe because they were meant for you, my Love. Thanks for bidding me farewell in that final dream on the morning of your departure when I saw you walking towards me with your legs having been healed by God as you put it. Indeed you had been healed because you did not need those earthen limbs anymore when you had received your spiritual ones ready to take you into your new life. There have been occasions when I find myself in a state I don't understand. Whilst lying in bed on my back, not sure whether I am awake or asleep, I see you leaning over me and kissing me good night. When I try to lift my arms to embrace you, they fail me. When I come to, you are gone. How I wish you would appear to me more often. I am convinced I will not run away from you as I badly need you. In any case, can an apparition really harm anyone?*

*Now I cherish the memories of our thirty years together, both the good and the bad. I badly miss what I then considered to be your nagging but in hind sight was clearly your expression of love and duty to our marriage. I know that I was not the exemplary husband you had always wished for but you continued to love and cherish me all the same. I take comfort in that you always forgave me and that God has also forgiven me. However, I wish you could now tell me if you were really human or an angel, for physically you were human while spiritually you were an angel.* **'An angelic being going through a human experience,'** *as young Frank Matenda would probably put it. It would now appear you have returned to where you really belong, among those of your kind. Please tell me why God had sent you to such a sinner. Have you now left me because I am incorrigible or because you have achieved your assignment? How I wish I had clarity on the way forward, on the plans that God has for me, for I am in limbo and terribly confused.*

*My Love, you were such an enigma, a puzzle that no human could solve. Despite the failure by everyone to understand you, you continued to appreciate and love us all. You remained gentle and caring. You were the Rose among other roses, the Rose of roses, and the Rose in perennial bloom, never to fade away, which the human eye failed to appreciate in preference to the seasonal one. While I mourn your departure, I celebrate your wonderful life with great hope. I know you had your weaknesses but you came as a package and given another chance, I will pick the same package all over again. Whilst on one hand I grieve, on the other I celebrate in the full knowledge that you are in your Creator's loving arms.*

*For a good thirty years you were my faithful companion and soul mate. You never tired from pointing the right direction. You were a giant at heart and yet I only saw it in flashes while most of the time I preferred to see a midget. You loved me without reservation and stuck with me both in good and in bad times. Clearly, you were specially tutored by angels while I was taught by the humans of this confused world, hence our differences.*

*I pray that God visits me in a special way so that I may learn from you, even though I may only accomplish a portion of what you did. May the same grace that he showed when he gave you to me continue to be visited upon me so that I don't go astray.*

**"Those who die in the Lord will rest from their labour and their works will follow them" Revelations 14 and verse 13.** *May your good soul indeed rest in peace and the good Lord of all grace give you comfort!*

*Once again, thanks for the children, my Love. How I wish they would all take after you, their beautiful mum. I know there is some good in me as well, which, when blended with yours, will make them*

soar high. May the good Lord be their permanent guide in the course
of their sojourn on this earth.

Thanks for everything my Love, my Rose… my everything.

Till we meet again, may your beautiful soul indeed rest in eternal
peace.

In everlasting love,
Your husband

Bryan
January 2008

## 23.4    Letter Four

Poem from Tatenda (Tee) composed and read at his mother's
funeral service.

### The Rose of all roses
It is no coincidence that our mother's name was Rose
Like a the flower in the gardens
Our mother was always beautiful and fully bloomed
So beautiful she was on this earth,
So beautiful she is in her resting place
If there is one thing I learnt from our mother in my 29 years on
earth
It was unconditional love.

### Dear Mother
Thank you for the love and guidance over the years
In life we loved you dearly
In death we do the same
It has broken our hearts to lose you
But we know that as long as we follow your legacy

*We will meet again*
*The day you left us,*
*You did not go alone:*
*For part of us went with you,*
*The day the Lord called your name*
*We love you.*

**Dear God**

*Thank you for giving us a mother like no other*
*On this day we ask you for a favour*
*We know that Roses grow in heaven, Lord*
*So please pick a bunch for us,*
*Place them in our mother's arms*
*And tell her that they are from her children*
*Tell her that we love her and miss her*
*And when she turns to smile*
*Please hold her for a while*
*Because remembering her is so easy,*
*We will do it everyday.*

*AMEN*

*Your loving son,*
*Tatenda*

## 23.5    Letter Five

Letter from Munya (*muroora)*

*Mum,*

*You were the greatest person I have ever known.*
*You were and still are exceedingly beautiful.*
*I got scared when Tatenda told me that you were literally good at anything you set yourself to do.*
*How will I ever cope staying with such a person, will I ever satisfy her, I asked myself.*
*I cannot stop playing back in my mind the first time I met you.*
*I had no idea how you would accept me and I was scared*
*But when you greeted me and gave me that hug you made all my fears go away.*
*You simply disarmed and assured me.*
*I knew right then that I would always be welcome and felt really comfortable around you.*
*Even when I used to call and speak to you on the phone, you always made me feel loved and welcome.*
*Your greeting words were always "Hi mwanangu, how are you."*
*There was never a day that I dreaded calling you because you were always a happy person and never complained a single day.*

*Even when I felt low, after speaking to you I would feel lifted.*
*You always would assure me that things would be okay and that it was just a matter of time, and you always reminded us to pray to God and that He would provide.*
*Now that you are no longer here with us, I feel sad, but happy at the same time because I know that you are always watching us from above.*

*I might not have done all that I would have wanted for you, but I am blessed to have spent the time I did with you and to have had you as my mum-in-law.*

*Now when I think of you, I smile and say that I must have been the luckiest "muroora" to have a mother-in-law who loved me the way you did. I never had anything bad to say about you, nor did I ever hear anything bad said about you, coz you were just amazing. You loved me like your own daughter and I am really blessed.*

*I miss you mum.*

*Munya*

## 23.6  Letter six

Letter from Tafadzwa Thelma (Fadzi)

*Mummy,*

*All I remember is sitting on my bed that fateful day I received the news, crying out to God asking why, not really understanding what it all meant. My heart pounding and my hands shaking, I remember thinking, "Not my mother, she can't be gone", but you were indeed gone and it hurt so much. I just could not believe it, and in that instance I felt like my world had crumbled.*

*I had intended to write both you and Daddy a letter just to thank you for the many things that you did for us. And for being just such wonderful parents, but as fate would have it I never got to write that letter, or to hear you say "Thank you dear" after reading it. Well here is a letter for you mummy; I know you can read this even though you are now a spirit.*

*I'll start by saying that NO one will EVER be able to replace you. Your beautiful soul, your tenacity and the kind of love you had for people will not be forgotten. You touched so many lives in so many ways and I am still amazed at the things you achieved in your short life on this earth. You were an amazing woman in my eyes, I want to thank you mummy for the Love you gave to us over the years, for showing us a kind of love that is unconditional and surpasses everything else. Not a day went by when you didn't do something loving for one if not all of us. Thank you for the sacrifices you made for us. Thank you for putting us first, even when things were not easy and for giving us a life that I can only hope to give my children some day, God willing.*

*Thank you for being such a strong, resilient woman. A woman who when faced with difficult situations and scenarios always kept her head up, never gave up and knew just what to do to get through it.. The strength you showed makes me feel like I can pull through anything. I love you for all you did for me as my mother. I have learnt a lot from you, so much so that it's hard to sum up in a letter. I'll never ever be able to understand the reason God saw it fit for you to leave this earth, but I know it was part of his plan and I'm so grateful to him for having given me a mother like you.*

*It's hard sometimes when I realise that I will NEVER just pick up the phone and hear your voice on the other end, I will NEVER hear you laughing or even just have you make us one of your most amazing meals. It's the little things that count and some days are harder than others, but with God's grace and love I know we'll be fine.*

*I know you're still watching over us from day to day while interceding for us to God and that we will never be apart in spirit. Don't worry about daddy; even though I know you look over him all the time. We will take care of him. We are a strong family and we will pull through it and make you so proud of us.*

*I have been saying a prayer for you every chance I get and I will continue to do so till that day we meet once again on that beautiful shore.*

*May the Lord God bless your beautiful and precious soul forever and ever....*

*Love you always*

*Your daughter,*
*Fadzi,*

## 23.7    Letter seven

From Kevin Tawanda (Bluz)

*Dear Mum,*

*I must have been 11-years-old when we were at Jomo Kenyatta International Airport heading back home to Zimbabwe after a two year stay in Kenya. The whole family was travelling except for you and Tee. You, as usual having an I-can-always-do-better attitude decided to stay back and learn the art of weaving and other handicrafts. The kiss you gave me on my cheek as you bid us farewell is what I've always carried with me. Eighty percent of the time we would argue and fight over something I had or hadn't done. That kiss was my understanding of what your love for me was.*

*Mum, your story is like no other, and just as much, my version is just one glimpse of a life story from just one angle. For people to truly understand, visualize and appreciate you and what you did whilst still alive, they will have to speak to the numerous souls that you touched when you walked the earth.*

*It had been five years since I had last seen you when you passed on and about four to six months since I had last spoken to you. The last word I last heard you say was "No..." after dad had asked you if you wanted to talk to me on the phone. You were crushed, just as much as he was when you heard that I had started smoking and drinking. You were obviously concerned for my health and well being.*

*Over the years I have heard the saying 'you don't know what you got till it's gone'. And with the risk of sounding generic with such a cliché, I will concur - I did not know. I took you and your love for granted. I think we all did.*

*Don't be fooled into thinking that all we see is all there is. Angels do walk this planet everyday and you were one of them. Those who knew you would tell of the miracles you performed. And by miracles, I don't mean the biblical type. I am talking about substantially helping over twenty people and putting my cousins through school while the whole time you never missed attending to us. I can never remember a time when we thought you neglected us.*

*The most amazing thing I have ever seen, more breath-taking than any landscape or sunset; is the amount of people who came to mourn you and give their testimonies on how you had helped them significantly in their lives, even strangers.*

*The hardest day of my life was when I received three calls from Simba, Fadzi and Lynda telling me what had happened. All phone calls came within the space of ten minutes. The first was to let me know of the accident and your critical condition. I would like to thank Simba for that call. The second was the same but felt harder and made me realize how critical the situation was. I'd like to thank Lynda, for that. The third came in the last minute of those ten. Fadzi called and was crying. I let her know that I had been told that our mom had been in an accident. She cried louder and told me that you had passed away. I would like to thank her for that too. I told her that*

*I would be there as soon as possible, put the phone down and cried like I have never done before. May God bless your soul, mum.*

*Mum, I miss you and I simply don't know how life will be without you. You were an angel I failed to recognize until you left us. Although it may now appear to be late, let me apologize for the heart ache and pain I caused you. I love you and I always will.*

*I have now learnt the following facts of life;*
*Never take family for granted*
*Never put friends in front of family*
*Understand family is home and home is where the heart is*
*When it's all said and done, the only one thing standing with you is family and You were the soul of that family*

*Mummy, I love you, always have and always will. I'm sorry for the arguments and fights. I am hard-headed and I remember you saying that we are both stubborn and that's why we never get along.*

*I would give anything to help you in the garden with your flowers again.*
*I know I did not live up to your expectations and yet you saw greatness in me but one day you are going to smile and be proud. You have taught us a lot, and with a risk of sounding bad, your death brought this family closer. It made us to understand how fragile life is and how we need to take care and love each other.*

*We love you, and will see you soon. Take care of us*

*Your most loving son*

*Kevin*
*P.S. we hope you liked the roses*

## 23.8    Letter eight

From Lynda Tariro (Lily)

*To mom*

*My friend's dad and uncle died in a car accident today mom, the same way I lost you;    the same way u were taken away. I thought it was all downhill from here but it brought everything back. Everything! Mom....I wish you were back. I don't want to pretend like you are just a memory, you gave me life but now I don't have you anymore....tears are streaming down my face, I'm not ok mom! I'm not! I need you, so-o-o much! I realize now that I never had anything to worry about when you were here; sure, we had our disagreements from time to time and I'd think to myself why can't she just leave me alone.*

*But now I don't want you to leave me alone anymore, mom! I don't.*

*It hurts too much!*

*I want you to call me from watching television and say "how many times have I told you to clean your room?" I want you to tell me to do the dishes even though everyone else is sitting around and I've been busy all day. I want you to ask me to make you a cup of tea when I'm watching my favourite TV show. I want to watch gardening shows with you and have you tell me how beautiful you think every plant is. I want you to look at me and say "really?" as you stand in front of the mirror after I tell you how lovely you looked; just so I could say yes, you looked lovely I want you to send me to the garden and get carrots/beans/peppers to give to anyone and everyone who visited us. I want you to ask me to go buy bread early in the morning. I want you to wake me up early in the morning on a Saturday so we can clean the carpets. I want you to take it out on me when you've had a bad day. You would bring me soup in my room after I told you I'm sick but I'll be fine mom don't worry. You would fall fast asleep a few minutes after sitting on the sofa coz you'd be exhausted,*

Because you would have been too busy doing things for everyone else. You would look at me when we were driving home and say "I know I probably shouldn't but....should we?" then I'd smile and say yes and we'd go to On the Run takeaway shop and order 2 large cones with chocolate flakes in them and sit in the car and eat them while talking about how good they were. I would say thanks mom and you would say "uchitendei nhai mwanangu"(don't mention my child). You would ask me everyday if it looked like your diet was working, if it looked like you were losing weight and all the while I'd be thinking 'mom, you're perfect no matter how much you weigh' Good Lord, what will I ever do... People may not know this but I struggled a lot as a teenager, something happened to me today mom and I wanted so badly to talk to you about it because I know you'd know just what to say. You and dad sent my brothers and sister to boarding school but decided to keep me at home. I was always alone and because of that I was sad but you were always there. It was because you always wanted me by you and I didn't realize how close we had become...I hadn't realized why you'd kept me near...because I was your baby... I finished high school and couldn't wait to leave the country like my elder siblings. I didn't manage to go to Canada and I was crushed so dad thought Australia was the next option but you suggested South Africa more than one time...why? I found out it was because you wanted me nearer home so I could visit home more often! Vimbayi, my friend, told me during your funeral that one day you told her mom that you were so happy that I didn't go to University straight after high school, and that I spent a full year with you before I eventually left. You have no idea what that meant to me. And that day at Church when I was saying my goodbyes to everyone and you looked at me and said,

"Wow, watching you say goodbye to everyone just made me realize, you really are going, I'm sad"...here I was trying to leave and you jus wanted to hold on to me.

So all the while I thought I was overprotected when you just didn't want me gone...but now you're gone...and you're not coming back. Why did I have to understand why you did what you did after

## 23.9    Letter nine

A condolence message from Crawley Church of Christ in The United Kingdom

The following are the words on the front cover of the condolence card received with appreciation from my good sisters, Merle and her daughter Sandy Baines from Crawley Church of Christ in the United Kingdom. I found the words to be very relevant and aptly describing the nature of Rose who grew up, lived and thrived in adversity but when an opportunity arose she passed on to the other side, where she is obviously appreciated more.

### *The Rose beyond the Wall*
*A rose once grew*
*Where all could see,*
*Sheltered behind a garden wall*
*And, as the days*
*Passed swiftly by,*
*It spread its branches*
*Straight and tall......*

*One day*
*A beam of light shone through*
*A crevice that had opened wide*
*The rose bent gently*
*Towards its warmth*
*Then passed beyond*
*To the other side........*

## 23.10    Avondale Church of Christ -Testimonies from the ladies

### 23.10.1   From Essie Naude

*Rose, you were a lovely lady. You were always so gentle and kind and giving. Thank you for the times we shared together. You will always be remembered for your motherly love and kindness you shared with your sisters in Christ.*

### 23.10.2 From Thulani Sibanda

*Rose was a friend, a sister and a role model for me. She was full of love, warmth and happiness. She was a very hardworking, caring wife and mother. I learnt a lot from Rose. She shared produce from her garden with all around her. I shared some dishes and recipes with her.*

*The last quality time that I had with Rose was when we travelled to Kwekwe for her sister-in-law's funeral. For the greater part of the journey, she shared with us some of her dreams and told us meanings for certain dreams. She talked about prayer and indicated to us that she really felt she was communicating with her heavenly father in those days. When we asked how she knew, she smiled and told us that she could see some light in her prayers.*

*May her soul rest in peace.*

### *23.10.3 From Nancy Ngorima*

*Rose was very generous; she used to bring vegetables to church for us to share and they were free of charge.*

*One day, after her serious illness in which she was nursed on oxygen therapy, she told me that she knew she was not going to die at that time.*

*Rose was very free to give other ladies recipes for cooking since she was one of the best cooks, e.g. she gave us her carrot cake recipe.*

*She also demonstrated flower arranging at one of the ladies' meetings.*

*On 24 November, 2007, I sat with Rose at the dinner we had at the home of the Magayas and as we were talking, we went to get our food together and we shared one of the dishes which was very delicious. We went back together for some more. That day there was a lot of singing and we really enjoyed our singing.*

*One day, in the morning, Rose called me on the telephone and told me that she wanted to sing with me the song that she had been singing in her vision or dream. She said she had been singing the song in her heart and requested me to join her as I knew the song. I complied and we sang over the telephone and she was very ecstatic about it.*

*Rose was a counsellor to young couples and was always there for my children's ups and downs. She was always the first point of call when my married daughter had problems at home. I often prayed with her for our children.*

*Rose was my colleague, a professional, and therefore, we used to encourage each other. I wonder why we nurses are not also resuscitated, yet we resuscitate others.*

*Rose, you were a hard worker. Rest in peace...*upiwe korona yako nokuti basa wakaita ukapedza *(you deserve your crown of righteousness).*

## 23.10.4 From Rosemary Tindwa

*Rose was extremely kind…she dropped by often on her way to work with carrots, vegetables, fresh corn when in season, or fresh honey for Joey and us as a family…she shared what she had.*

*Rose had a servant's heart…for example, just a month before her death, as we talked about her studies over the phone, I mentioned that I was taking care of Joey in the absence of house-help and was going to leave him with the gardener to attend to something pressing. Rose was so concerned about the arrangement and Joey's safety that she offered to forego her time in the library to come and stay with Joey. Although I did not let her, the offer mirrored her selflessness and servant heart.*

*Rose was humble…she served the Lord in situations that would not put her in the limelight, e.g. when we asked her to be an MC at a ladies' prayer seminar, she garnered every excuse she could think of, but was glad to be responsible for seating arrangements where she would not be noticed.*

*Rose opened her home to so many of her husband's relatives that she was a challenge and example to many of us ladies at Avondale Church, because she did it with joy and without grumbling.*

*Confidentiality: those who confided in Rose testified that she was one to keep people's confidence.*

*Rose opened her home to ministry…many church guests were hosted by the Matutus.*

*Rose depended on the Lord…this was reflected by her requests for prayer and her testimonies of God's working in her life as she experienced him at a personal level.*

*Rose had that quiet and gentle spirit…that soft laughter by which she exuded the joy of the Lord and that inner beauty that only comes with intimacy with God.*

*Rose loved her husband dearly; she strove to make Bryan comfortable and take care of his needs…for example, at fellowship lunches, Rose checked out the foods that were suitable for "B" as she fondly referred to him. What an example to all of us married women!*

*Rose was industrious...very gifted with her hands and always trying something to supplement her income or better herself...quite a Proverbs 31:10-31 woman.*

*Thank you, Lord, for allowing us to know Rose and to share in celebrating her life, but most of all, thank you for the assurance that those who die in Christ have eternal life...'O death, where is your sting...?' 1 Cor 15:55*

## 23.10.5 From Alice Mhlanga

*I first knew Rose in 1988 when her family moved from Rusape to Harare because of Bryan's work promotion.*

*The Matutus found residence in Sunridge just blocks away from our home in Greencroft. We bonded as families right away.*

*Rose found employment at Chitungwiza Hospital. She soon embarked on a nursing course that saw her being up-graded to a Registered nurse. She worked hard to attain this and achieved flying colours in one or two of her courses.*

*Rose was a neat person and her home showed how industrious she was...a neat garden, flourishing pot plants and a tidy house. If she passed by our place and saw a plant she admired she would take a shoot (cutting) to plant at her home and I would do the same if I passed by her place. She was so generous in her giving and she gave from her heart. She was fond of plants and flowers and we decided to take a flower arranging course together. Whatever she did, Rose did it with all her heart, striving to bring excellence out of it. The book of Proverbs makes it clear that diligence – being willing to work hard and doing one's best at any job given to him or her, is a vital part of wise living. Rose was a good example of Proverbs' teachings.*

*Rose had outstanding abilities, using her hands and resources to make the best of every situation. In Sunridge, she took in Bryan's younger brothers who were taking various courses and treated them as her own children, just as she did with numerous nephews and nieces who stayed in her home in later years. She became an excellent mother to them.*

*Rose was humble and gentle. I believe that her strength and dignity did not come from her amazing achievements but were a result of her reverence for God. I also believe that her attractiveness to the people around her came entirely from her character, a woman who was not proud of what she had achieved or who she was. I believe she knew where all blessings came from. From Rose, we all learned the virtues of industriousness, integrity and resourcefulness. I salute her for what she was to us during her short life here on earth."*

## 23.10.6 From Carolyn Chetsanga

*When I think of Rose, I reflect on the beauty of the flower that bears her name. In every way, Rose Matutu was as lovely to behold and a joy to those who knew her and shared experiences with her.*

*The beauty and abundance of the well-tended roses in Rose's garden bore testimony to her love of gardening. Her garden behind the house produced vegetables and fruits of all kinds and she generously shared the produce with her friends.*

*I remember admiring flourishing strawberry plants and their fruits in her garden one day. I recounted my sad efforts at growing strawberries that year from stock given to me by another friend. Rose gave me some advice on growing strawberries and asked if I wanted more plants; she needed to clear out some plants from her garden and I could take a dozen or so. The gardener was tasked with clearing out the excess strawberry plants and setting them aside for me. When I collected the plants later and set them out in my own garden, I discovered that I had been given about 50 strawberry plants! With the good, healthy stock from Rose's garden and her expert advice on growing strawberries, I expanded my own strawberry patch over the next couple of years. When Rose lamented one day that her gardener had allowed all of her strawberry plants to die from neglect, I was able to return the favour and I sent Rose as many plants from our garden so that she could replant her beds.*

*Rose was a capable and caring teacher of the young children at Avondale Church. Year after year, Rose volunteered to teach the very young children, even during the last few years of her life when she was studying day and night for her degree. Whenever her studies kept Rose from coming to church on Sunday morning, she arranged for someone to take her class. She nurtured the young and older children at church as much as she did the plants in her garden, feeding them lessons from the Word of God.*

*Rose was very industrious. Throughout the years that I knew her, she was always working on some project, be it curtains for the house, tending her garden, providing hospitality to relatives and friends from church, learning to arrange flowers, cooking and baking for church lunches, teas and bake sales, studying to complete her A-levels, then working on a university degree program in the last couple of years in addition to holding a challenging and responsible position with Premier Medical Aid Society.*

*Above all, Rose loved her family and raised her children "in the fear and admonition of the Lord." Kevin and Lynda, the two younger children, participated actively in the Vacation Bible School programs as puppeteers. Lynda continued the tradition and taught a Bible Class until she also departed to study overseas. When all of the children had left home to study and live abroad, Rose kept in constant touch with them by telephone and e-mail. She loved to share news from each of the children and her face would light up when asked about any or all of them.*

*Her husband, Bryan, had special dietary needs and Rose spent time and energy to ensure that he ate nourishing food that did not upset his digestive system.*

*I thank God for granting me the privilege of knowing and loving a special rose from his garden, Rose Matutu."*

# 24

# Lessons from the Rose Garden

*"To everything there is a season, a time for everything under the sun; A time to be born and a time to die ..." so says Ecclesiastes chapter 3 verses 1 and 2.*

One day, my good friend and brother, Eubert and I were debating why misfortunes befall both the righteous and the unrighteous alike, like in the case of Job. Why did God not discriminate in favour of the righteous, we asked. A suggestion was made that probably God in his wisdom, in creating nature, did it in such a way that nature was given the autonomy to regulate itself without his daily intervention. Instead of God having to ensure that a particular river takes a given course to the sea, he allows it to chart its own course even if it means that other forms of life are destroyed in the process. Hence the ecological balancing acts of nature. Human activities like the uncontrolled burning of fossil fuels, among many others, interfere with the ozone layer resulting in global warming and its related consequences. An angry volcano and a tsunami rising from the sea are the results of some imbalances somewhere and are meant to correct those imbalances. When the 2km wide and 300m deep Mt. Kilimanjaro crater was formed by vicious volcanic eruptions many, many centuries ago, those who may have witnessed the phenomenon would never have known that later generations would find pleasure and marvel at its grandeur. Then, it caused untold damage to life but now it sustains the successors to that very life.

In the process of such activities, lots of lives, both flora and fauna, are destroyed. Consequently, fresh imbalances arise until eventually; there is tranquillity when the balance is regained. God would therefore not interfere, although he can if he so wishes, as the laws governing those forces have already been put in place. The negative effects are therefore not directly of God's making but of contravening the laws governing the systems that he has put in place. Believing otherwise would be like someone breaking the law and blaming the legislators of that country for passing that law in the first place.

Accordingly, the accident that took Rose could have been the consequence of the fact that Rose had gone for some days with inadequate sleep and was progressively getting tired up to the day of the accident. In this case, the laws of nature that require us to have rest would have been contravened. While God could have prevented the accident if he had wished so, he had no obligation to do so. It is in this light therefore, that I accept that my wife's time for departure from this earth was up and that the forces of nature played their part using the laws bequeathed to them by the Almighty God. The season for death had arrived for her and there was nothing she or anyone could have done about it.

On 1 March 1953, God planted a beautiful Rose in his garden. The Rose flourished as he nourished and cared for it jealously. The Rose, which was always in bloom, had a beautiful scent that permeated all its surroundings. While other roses around it acquired the qualities of this Rose, others failed dismally although they were trying, some genuinely and others not quite so. When the Rose was at its peak, the forces of nature took their toll resulting in some imbalances and its uprooting for higher glory. It is my prayer that when balance returns, all the other roses will have learned to survive on their own without the scent and support from the blooming Rose.

What is left for me, my children and those around us is to glean some lessons from the blooming Rose and trust that God will guide and prosper us appropriately. Herewith, without discounting her weaknesses, some of the great lessons we have learnt from the Blooming Rose; God's Rose, my Rose.

## Fear of God

"Teach me your way, O Lord; I will walk in your truth. Unite my heart to fear your name." Psalm 86:11

"And His mercy is on those who fear Him from generation to generation." Luke 1:50

## Love

"The stranger who dwells among you shall be to you as one born among you, and you shall love him as yourself; for you were a stranger in the land of Egypt." Leviticus 19:34

"A new commandment I give to you, that you love one another: as I have loved you, that you may also love one another." John 13:34

## Humility

"But who am I and who are my people that we should be able to give so willingly as this? For all things come from you, and of your own have we given you." 1 Chronicles 29:14

"If I then, your Lord and teacher, have washed your feet, you also aught to wash one another's feet." John 13:14

## Honesty
"You shall have honest scales, and an honest bath." Ezekiel 45:10

"Providing honourable things, not only in the sight of the Lord, but also in the sight of men." 2 Corinthians 8:21

## Generosity
"Cast your bread upon the waters, for you will find it after many days. Give a serving to seven and also to eight, for you do not know what evil will be on the earth." Ecclesiastes 11:1, 2

"But whoever has this world's goods and sees his brother in need, and shuts up his heart from him, how does the love of God abide in him?" 1 John 3:17

## Forgiveness
"Do not rejoice when your enemy falls, and do not let your heart be glad when he stumbles." Proverbs 24:17

"Bless those who persecute you, bless and do not curse." Romans 12:14

## Industry/diligence
"Do not love sleep, lest you come to poverty; open your eyes and you shall be satisfied with bread." Proverbs 20:13

"That you also aspire to lead a quiet life, to mind your own business, and to work with your own hands, as we commanded you." 1 Thessalonians 4:11. See also 2 Thessalonians 3:8, 9

## Perseverance

"The Lord is good to those who wait for him, to the soul who seeks him. It is good that one should hope and wait quietly for the salvation of the Lord." Lamentations 3:25, 26

"For this reason I also suffer these things; nevertheless I am not ashamed, for I know whom I have believed and am persuaded that he is able to keep what I have committed to Him until that day." 2 Timothy 1:12

## Commitment

"But Ruth said; 'entreat me not to leave you, or to turn back from following after you; for wherever you go, I will go. Wherever you lodge I will lodge. Your people shall be my people, and your God, my God. Where you die, I will die and there will I be buried. The Lord do so to me and more also, if anything but death parts you and me'". Ruth 1:16, 17,

"But Ittai answered the king and said; 'As the Lord lives and as the lord my king lives, surely in whatever place my lord the king shall be, whether in death or life, even there also your servant will be.'" "2 Samuel 15:21

"I beseech you therefore brethren, by the mercies of God, that you present your bodies a living sacrifice, holy, acceptable to God, which is your reasonable service." Romans 12:1

## Service and loyalty.

"And if it seems evil to you to serve the Lord, choose this day who you will serve, whether the gods which your fathers served on the other side of the river or the gods of the Amorites, in whose lands you dwell. But as for me and my house, we will serve the Lord." Joshua 24: 15

"Yet it shall be so among you: but whoever desires to become great among you, let him be your servant. And whoever desires to be first among you, let him be your slave." Matthew 20: 26, 27.

By coming up with these quotations to illustrate Rose's personality, I am not saying that she excelled in all of them. Indeed, she had her shortcomings, like we all have ours. Suffice it to say, one way or another, her life taught us something about these virtues; for that is the gist of my message. May all glory be given to the Almighty God for the inspiration I got when writing this book.

May the Almighty indeed bless everyone who reads this book.

# 25

## Further Lessons from the Rose Garden

I have come up with these thoughts and conclusions after observing life in general and on reflecting on Rose's life in particular. Some are therefore general while others relate specifically to her life. My personal relationship with God and the special favours he has bestowed upon me, despite being a sinner, have had a major impact on my outlook on life. If there are any similarities with other people's work, it is entirely unintended and purely coincidental.

I suggest that the reader meditates on any two sayings per weak and see how these apply to daily life. These will therefore take 52 weeks to go through and by then a new cycle would begin. One should never tire of them because they are practical and put our lives into perspective. When all has been said and done, one will be able to appreciate how, although very small in God's scheme of things, the human being remains the most favoured of His earthly creations.

## A) Health issues

1. Avoid sneezing, cough instead; sneezing is bad for sinuses and the rib cage and invariably causes headaches while coughing clears the lungs and relieves the throat.

2. Many a times we suffer from physical ailments because we do not listen to our bodies; a body is a very intricate system that always shouts out its likes and dislikes, listen and live.

3. The inability by man to fully exploit nature's self healing capacity is the biggest blemish on human ingenuity.

4. While we continue to break the laws of nature with reckless abandon and with devastating consequences to our health, our quest for physical salvation from the same nature, the very source of our life and sustenance, is rather muted.

5. Excessive pain may be better than no pain at all, for one who has gone through such an experience can only be wiser than the one who has not.

6. Unexplained pain is usually a symptom; it is unadvisable to take pain killers unless the pain is unbearable.

## B) Love and Justice

7. While it is always blessed to give; giving without desire and affordability is not only unproductive but also counter productive.

8. It is noble and more rewarding to celebrate the quality of one's work rather than the quantity of one's profit.

9.    Admission of one's wrong is a lot wiser than bragging about one's right

10.   Love and generosity provide nutrition to the heart.

11.   Human endeavour is sweeter and more fulfilling where there is no malice.

12.   Sharing without love is empty.

13.   Sharing is the most fulfilling experience one can ever have; for one who cannot share cannot belong.

14.   Sharing should not be determined by extent of one's material possessions but by the size of one's heart.

15.   Love is not transient and will never be.

16.   Kindness, when well intended, can be addictive.

17.   Generosity, of necessity, is like one-way traffic; it does not depend on reciprocity.

18.   Expression of gratitude should by itself not be a solicitor for further favours.

19.   Justice is like air, without it we suffocate.

20.   Even the poorest person on earth has something to give; love.

21.   Wealth is largely tangible perception while love is largely intangible reality; sadly humans prefer tangibility over intangibility and perception over reality.

22. A gram of love weighs far much more than a tonne of wealth.

23. If we could all be able to forgive and forget, paradise would be restored.

## C) Life and Death

24. We are who we are not because we are clever, but because we have a destiny.

25. The grave is not the final resting place; it is the only resting place.

26. As stubborn as the truth; one can always twist and stretch lies without limit but the truth will always remain stubbornly unmoved.

27. Separating man from his culture can be severely traumatic; it is like separating the spiritual from the physical.

28. We are consumed as we brood today over yesterday's events for tomorrow's sake to no avail.

29. We are all opportunists; what differs is the extent of our greed.

30. We cry for and write to the departed for our selfish reasons.

31. Life and death are two sides of the same coin; one cannot exist without the other.

32. The only two universal languages are birth and death; anyone who claims to speak any other is a liar.

33.  Just as we pay instalments towards our long term debts, we also pay instalments towards our burial by depositing bits and pieces of our bodies into the ground during our lifetime.

34.  We never get used to death, not because it is new but because it always takes a new person.

35.  It is selfish to decree that one should not be mourned, for by so doing, one is denying the living their turn to be selfish.

36.  I want to go back to my roots because my roots are anchored in Mother Earth.

37.  I am not ugly, I am not beautiful, I am human; that is my only distinction from other creatures.

38.  Ugliness and beauty do not exist but, like everything else that we know, are functions of our skewed values.

39.  Tampering with the physical attributes of our bodies is like environmental degradation, natural disasters are bound to follow.

40.  My physical attributes, like my skin colour, hair texture and nose, are a result of adaptation to the land of my forefathers; they are a blessing.

## D) The Almighty God

41.  If God did not want the human species to multiply, he would not have given us the capacity to do so; that is why our efforts to the contrary are futile.

42. When God created the world He also put in motion natural laws to govern it; expecting God to prevent draughts or floods is like expecting the chief executive of a company to clean the toilet.

43. Both natural and manmade disasters, including aircraft crashes and earthquakes, tend to occur one after another; it is because forces of imbalance would have been triggered and it takes time for balance to be restored.

44. Raising children is a God given responsibility; we should neither wrap them in cotton wool nor spread for them a bed of thorns. (Influenced by M K Gandhi)

45. Although God will destroy this world, it is man's greed that will be the catalyst.

46. The social and emotional aspects of marriage should be in aid of the physical and the spiritual; for that is all there is about God.

47. Marriage is a form of worshipping God

48. God created us for the sole purpose of worshiping him; his insurance policy is our ability to reproduce.

49. By creating us mortal, God probably knew that we would otherwise be conceited.

50. Marriage is never by accident even where it fails; some souls are always blessed.

51. The end of a terrestrial human life is the beginning of a celestial one; we should always celebrate.

52. The only way God reacts viciously to assaults on him is when he responds to environmental degradation by man.

53. Everyone is a child of God; it is only that some prefer to be orphans.

54. Had God created more than two sexes, instances of homosexuality would probably have been reduced.

55. If I had two eyes and everyone else had been created with one, I would be abnormal.

56. No matter how hopeless one's offspring are, there is a need to count one's blessings; God speaks to us through them.

57. A new birth brings joy to the living and cries to the new arrival while death brings joy to the newly departed and cries to the living.

58. The horizon may be out of physical reach but it is real, and so is heaven.

59. Answers are like God, they are always there; they only need to be sought.

60. Every circumstance, no matter how adverse, is an opportunity for worshipping God

61. God is the master craftsman; he gave me a mouth that fits my nose, eyes that fit my forehead and feet that can carry my weight; who am I to tamper with his model.

62. Just as I cannot say one baboon is more beautiful than the other, the same applies to God in relation to humans; baboons are baboons and humans are humans, simple.

63. Marriage is like a long journey, the one who gets tired first before destination tends to be hurt the most.

64. My childhood impression of God; an old and benevolent bearded man whose flesh is made of a glowing, semi fluid precious substance that enables him to flow to any part of the world instantly when needed.

## E) Liars and Cowards

65. Liars are like a plague, without them life will be too predictable.

66. Racists are the dumbest people ever; they segregate themselves from those they consider inferior whilst they share the air they inhale with them.

67. Insolence is the refuge of cowards.

68. Hatred and jealousy consume the perpetrator rather than the victim.

69. Cruel people are the most cowardly; reverse the roles and see how pathetic they become.

70. Cruelty is invariably a cover for cowardice, otherwise why would cruel people almost always attack the weaker party.

71. War is the ultimate expression of cowardice; for without cowards there is no war.

72. War is a game of babies; it is based on fantasies and there is rarely a winner

73.  Politics is an honourable occupation involving dishonourable individuals.

## F) Human Temporality

74.  While entrepreneurship is natural to some people, to others it is as strange as fiction.

75.  How can I claim to read another person's mind when mine changes subject every five seconds.

76.  The fact that some of the things we do as soon as we come into this world is to cry and defecate does not mean that we are all well experienced in those matters.

77.  Infidelity and promiscuity are the worst forms of witchcraft ever known to man.

78.  Cry with those laughing and laugh with those crying, for that is the only way to moderate excesses.

79.  Going against the grain may be painful but often achieves the desired results.

80.  Heroes are not only unsung, they can't sing.

81.  Love and hatred, like other forms of selfishness, are the major motivators of all human endeavours.

82.  Grass is green, glass is clear, class is fake.

83.  The eagle soars so high because it has high aspirations.

84.  Learning is neither an end in itself nor a means to an end; there is no end.

85.    One-way communications always entraps the recipient, whatever the nature of the news.

86.    Failure to flex is a recipe for breakage.

87.    That we have a destiny is not in dispute, the uncertainty is in its nature.

88.    If we were able to determine our fate we would determine the circumstances of our birth.

89.    We cope not because we want to, but because it is expedient to do so.

90.    For humans to live, both in this world and in the after-life, the body must be the slave of the soul; a reversal of roles will see both perish.

91.    Just as the body needs a balanced diet, so does the soul.

92.    At birth my age was 0% of my father's, who was 20 years old. At 20 I was 50% of his age. At 80 I will be 80% of my father's age and given long life, at this progression I will be close to 100% of my father's age at some point.

## G) Women

93.    Women are by instinct mothers first and wives second while men are children first and husbands second; both tend to spend inordinate amounts of time in their primary roles.

94.    Husbands are their wives' first born sons; any attempt to resist that by either party often results in a dysfunctional marriage.

95. God created us man and woman for balance; a world of women will be so full of caution that nothing would be done while that of man would be so reckless nothing would be effective.

96. A woman is nothing but God's special vessel; unfortunately that vessel often gets abused.

97. Despite protestations to the contrary, men are on average emotionally weaker than women; that is why men tend to resort to physical strength in order to win an argument.

## H) Children

98. One who is good at disciplining children is one without any children of his own (a Shona proverb).

99. A child is a gift from God and is, like any other gift, a cause for celebration; the absence of a gift is therefore no cause for despondency.

100. Had my mother practiced family planning resulting in me not being born, I would not have minded at all; I would not be there to mind.

101. Children are gifts, we get them at the discretion of the giver, solicited or not.

102. If animals fight to protect their offspring, humans should die in protection of theirs.

103. If having children was entirely by choice, at some point humans would be extinct.

# Glossary

Glossary of Zimbabwean names and nouns used in this book

| Name/noun | Meaning ( all names are in Shona language unless otherwise stated) |
|---|---|
| *Amai* | mother |
| *Amaiguru* | Elder brother's wife or mother's elder sister. Literally means older mother |
| *Amainini* | Mother's younger sister or *babamunini's* wife both meaning younger mother. It also means a man's younger brother's wife |
| *Amase* | Cottage cheese-like milk (Ndebele/Zulu |
| *Ambuya* | Grandmother. Also used affectionately for addressing old ladies |
| *Babakazi* | Father's sister literally meaning female father (Ndebele) |
| *Babamkhulu* | Grandfather (Ndebele/Zulu) |
| *Babamukuru* | Father's older brother or *maiguru's* husband, both meaning older father. Also means a woman's elder sister's husband |
| *Babamunini* | Father's young brother or *amainini's* husband both meaning younger father. Also means a woman's younger sister's husband |
| *Biravira* | One who is light in complexion or the bright one |
| *Chiedza* | Light |

| | |
|---|---|
| *Chigavakava* | Aloe, bitterness |
| *Chingarande* | The tough one. The rough rider |
| *Chiromonye* | One with a small mouth |
| *Dovorogwa* | The only child |
| *Fadzi* | Short version for Tafadzwa |
| *Gapiro* | The daring one |
| *Gogo* | Grandmother (Ndebele/Zulu) |
| *Hanzvadzi* | Sibling of opposite sex |
| *Hlupeko* | Child born after a lot of perseverance , usually after hope had been lost |
| *Hyanai* | Respect one another |
| *Hodzeko* | Cottage cheese-like milk |
| *Idombo* | Mediator between a man and prospective parents-in-law (Ndebele) |
| *Kudakwashe* | The Lord's will |
| *Kupusa* | Docility |
| *Kuzivakwashe* | The Lord knows why and how |
| *Kwazinkosi* | Same as *Kuzivakwashe* (Ndebele) |
| *MaNcube* | Affectionate name given to a maiden of the Ncube totem, used either before or after marriage. No age restriction. (Ndebele/Zulu) |
| *Mangwanani* | Morning or greeting as in good morning |
| *MaNdlovu* | Similar to *MaNcube* except this is for the Ndlovu (elephant) totem (Ndebele/Zulu). See also MaMpofu |
| *Manheru* | Evening or greeting as in good evening |

| | |
|---|---|
| *Mashakada* | Meal made of roughly crushed maize grain, boiled and mixed with peanut butter source (Shona/Ndebele) |
| *Mashavidze* | One who provides for and blesses others |
| *Masikati* | Afternoon or greeting as in good afternoon |
| *Matutu* | The Shona version of *Ndlela*, totem of the author. Alternatively spelt *"Mathuthu"* which is Shona spelt in Ndebele. Other variables are *Matsheza, Mugombi, Nhenga*. Relates to a kangaroo like hare called a spring hare. |
| *Mavhuna* | The tough one who breaks things |
| *Mbirashava* | Place of brown rock rabbits |
| *Mbuya* | Grandmother |
| *Mhembedzo* | Cause for celebration. My father was born when his own father was old, like in case of Isaac, as he had no children from first wife |
| *Mokoena* | Totem of the people related to the crocodile (Sotho). Same as Ngwenya (Ndebele) |
| *Mhofu* | Totem of people related to the Eland |
| *Mpofu* | Same as Mhofu (Ndebele) |
| *Mukoma* | Older sibling of same sex |
| *Mukwasha* | Son-in-law |
| *Munin'gina* | Younger sibling of same sex |
| *Munyaradzi* | Comforter |
| *Munyayi* | Mediator between a man and prospective parents-in-law |
| *Muroora* | Daughter-in-law |

| | |
|---|---|
| *Mutakura* | Meal made of boiled beans or peanuts, often mixed with maize grain |
| *Ndebele* | The language spoken by the largest minority of Zimbabwe's inhabitants which is a dialect of Zulu |
| *Muzukuru* | Nephew or grandchild of either sex |
| *Mwana'ngu* | My child |
| *Ndlela* | Author's totem which simply means "way or path". (Zulu) |
| *Nhopi* | Porridge made of boiled melon and maize meal |
| *Nkosana* | Prince (Zulu) |
| *Rupiza* | Edible sauce made of roasted beans, crushed to powder, boiled and mixed with peanut butter |
| *Sadza* | Thick porridge made of maize powder, a staple food for most people of Southern Africa |
| *Sekuru* | Grandfather or mother's brother |
| *Shona* | The language spoken by the majority of Zimbabwe's inhabitants |
| *Sibonile* | We have seen/noted |
| *Simba* | Short version for *Simbarashe* |
| *Simbarashe* | God's power |
| *Sitembile* | We are hopeful (Ndebele/Zulu) |
| *Sitshekwana* | Something out of focus or skewed. (Zulu/Ndebele) |
| *Tafadzwa* | We are very pleased |
| *Tanaka* | We are now fine with this addition to the family |

| | |
|---|---|
| *Tariro* | Hope |
| *Tatenda* | We are very grateful |
| *Tawanda* | A welcome addition to the family |
| *Thulani* | Please be quiet or let peace prevail (Ndebele) |
| *Tinashe* | God is with us |
| *Totem* | Most Bantu people of Southern Africa are 'related' to an animal or object which they consider sacred.<br>In many instances, they cannot touch or eat it. For example, the *Ngwenyas* normally don't eat any flesh from the water. Those of the Ncube totem would not eat/touch monkeys and baboons. |
| *Umcaba* | Meal made of hard boiled but crushed sorghum mixed with *amase (Zulu/ Ndebele* |
| *Umkhwenyana* | Son in law (Zulu/Ndebele) |
| *Umxhanxa* | Meal made of boiled mixture of maize grain and melon (Ndebele) |
| *VaGapiro* | Va denotes the royal plural and is added to one's name to show respect, especially the elderly or those in positions of authority. Such names are either derived from one's totem like in VaMaSibanda and VaGutu or real name like in VaChiromonye or even a nick name like in VaGapiro. This applies to both male and female. |
| *Vakoma* | Plural of *mukoma* |
| *Vanin'gina* | Plural of *munin'gina* |
| *Varoora* | Plural for daughter in law |

| | |
|---|---|
| *Vatete* | Father's sister(literally female father) or husband's sister |
| *Vazukuru* | Grandchildren or nephews (plural for *muzukuru*) |
| *Zulu* | A major language or tribe of South Africa |
| *Zvishavane* | Place of brown or golden soils |
| *Zviyo or rukweza* | Rapoko, a small red grain low in starch |

# About the author

Bryan Matutu was born on 28 May 1952 at Chiromonye Village in the Zvishavane district in the southern part of Zimbabwe. He did his primary and secondary education at Bilashaba Primary and Dadaya Secondary schools respectively between 1959 and 1971.

Bryan started his working career in a tyre manufacturing factory before joining the banking world in 1975. He served in the banking industry for 29 years until 2006 when he went on early retirement.

Born to a 'lay' preacher father who, unfortunately later fell by the wayside, Bryan was baptized into the Associated Churches of Christ (Christian Churches) whilst in high school, but only became a practicing Christian later in 1988. In 1977 he got married to Rose Sibusisiwe, a former childhood classmate. They had four children, two boys and two girls. While they had their share of the usual marital problems, the couple had a very rewarding marriage spanning a period of 30 years, only being separated by the death of Rose on 3 December 2007. The death of Rose brought a new perspective to Bryan's life culminating in his decision to write this book. Whilst he had always appreciated Rose during the subsistence of their marriage a new twist was brought into focus. His motivation in writing the book is simply to tell the story of Rose to the world and to celebrate what he considers to have been a remarkable life.

Bryan was first ordained as an elder in the Church of Christ at The Great Commission Church of Christ, Nairobi West in

1994. In 1999, he was once again ordained as an elder at Avondale Church of Christ at Avondale. However, he has since resigned for personal reasons. His strengths as an elder are in counseling across the age divide with a special focus on marriage related and youth matters.

Bryan also enjoys observing various forms of life and putting meanings to the phenomena affecting them. His exposure in banking where he dealt with people from all walks of life and where he acquired several qualifications in finance and management, and his eldership in the Church, have adequately equipped him to write this book. His three favourite books of the Bible, not in any order, are;

- Ecclesiastes: for King Solomon's philosophical debate on life and the beautiful conclusion.

- The Gospel according to Apostle John: for Jesus' wonderful discourse with his disciples starting from Chapter 14 and the promises contained therein.

- Apostle Paul's letter to the Philippians: for Paul's confidence in his relationship with his maker and the encouragement he gives to Christians of all generations that they can also attain that level of confidence.

It is Bryan's wish and prayer that all those who read this book will be blessed by the Almighty.

Bryan is contactable by email on bmatutu@africaonline. co.zw or telephone numbers +263 4 850730, +to 263 11 440909 and +263 912 932012